Totally Bound Publishing books by Molly Ann Wishlade:

Desire in Deadwood

The Duggans of Montana Volume One
Harlot at the Homestead
A Rancher for Rosie

I0663217

THE DUGGANS OF MONTANA
Volume One

Harlot at the Homestead

A Rancher for Rosie

MOLLY ANN WISHLADE

The Duggans of Montana Volume One
ISBN # 978-1-78430-703-5
©Copyright Molly Ann Wishlade 2015
Cover Art by Posh Gosh ©Copyright August 2015
Interior text design by Claire Siemaszkiewicz
Totally Bound Publishing

Published in 2015 by Totally Bound Publishing, Newland House, The Point, Weaver Road, Lincoln, LN6 3QN, United Kingdom.

HARLOT AT THE HOMESTEAD

Dedication

This one is dedicated to two very strong and special women.

Firstly, my lovely little Welsh Granny. Thank you for all those magical afternoons, when we sat together in front of your tiny portable TV and watched wonderful Westerns. I miss you so much but I treasure our memories. Love you!

Secondly, thanks to my fabulous editor, Sue. Without you, I might still be aspiring. You have taught me so much — I'm still learning — and I will be eternally grateful. Big hugs, lovely! xxx

Chapter One

"Kenan!" The cry pierced the night like a flaming arrow. "Help me!"

Kenan jumped to his feet, instantly alert. Just moments ago he'd been slumped in the fireside chair, losing the battle against exhaustion as the rain pattering against the windows and the crackling of the fire had lulled him to sleep. After two months on the cattle trail, he'd been relieved to be back at the Duggan homestead and his mind and body had begun to unwind.

But someone needed help. He grabbed his gun belt from the floor by the chair and fastened it around his waist.

"Kenan!" The anguished cry came again, carried on a voice filled with pain and fear.

He turned to check on his siblings, but the three of them stood wide-eyed and pale behind him like unearthly specters haunting the dimly lit room.

So who, on earth, had called him?

"Kenan, what was that?" Rosie rushed to his side and took hold of his arm. The alarm in her amber eyes was echoed in his racing heartbeat.

"It sounded like…" He squeezed his twin sister's hand. "Like…but it can't be."

There was a thud from outside as something landed on the wooden porch. Kenan took hold of Rosie's shoulders and pushed her back toward their two younger brothers.

"Stay here," he growled.

As he turned and walked toward the door, he removed his gun from its holster. He held it steady in his right hand and placed his left one on the door handle.

"Matthew, keep Rosie and Emmett well back."

Matthew nodded his dark head, his own gun already cocked.

Kenan released the catch and slowly opened the door, letting in the black night, the rain and a dead woman.

"Dear Lord in Heaven!" Rosie appeared at Kenan's side as he lifted the inanimate woman in his arms and carried her toward the warmth of the fire. She was drenched and ice cold. He laid her on the rag rug in front of the hearth and gazed at her.

"Kenan?" Rosie patted his shoulder and he stared into her bewildered eyes.

"It can't be."

Matthew knelt at Kenan's side and frowned at the sight before him. "How…why…I mean…"

Kenan shook his head. "I have no idea but she's soaked through and most likely has a fever." His thudding heart threatened to explode at any moment and as he reached out to smooth back the girl's sodden red hair, his hands trembled violently.

This didn't make any sense.

He couldn't fathom how or why, but Catherine Montgomery, the fiancée he'd grieved for the past two years, had appeared out of the blue at his homestead. His mind raced with unanswered questions but a flicker of hope sparked deep in his gut. He realized that in spite of his uncertainty and regardless of his fears, he was darned glad to see her — the woman he'd thought he would never see again.

"We'd better get her out of these wet things." Rosie nudged Kenan's shoulder.

"Yeah...of course." He leaned over and lifted the unconscious woman from the hearth.

She was as light as lamb's wool and blossoming warmth seeped through her damp clothing. Everywhere their bodies touched, his skin burned like it had been seared with a white-hot poker. He'd dreamt of holding her in his arms so many times and he'd even made silent promises to whatever deity existed that he'd ask no questions if she could just reappear in his life. But now that she had, Kenan was aware that he had a whole barrel full of questions that couldn't remain unanswered.

"Take her through to my room," Rosie whispered.

Kenan walked slowly, careful not to bump Catherine's feet against the table or the door frames. He looked down into her beautiful pale face and savored the beauty of her petite freckled nose and her coral rosebud mouth. Suddenly, she opened her eyes wide. She frowned for a moment then her pupils enlarged and Kenan's heart leaped with a mixture of love and fear. She'd come back from the dead but how and why? And what had happened to her?

"Kenan," she croaked and lifted a tiny hand to touch his face. Her fingertips were ice cold and for a moment he wondered if she really was dead — a spirit come to haunt him. Or had his grief finally become too much and his mind cracked with the sheer agony of it all? Maybe insanity would offer him some relief from the daily suffering he endured every time Catherine crossed his mind.

"Put her onto the bed." Rosie directed him.

He considered refusing and holding onto her, never letting her go again, but she was cold and wet and he realized how ridiculous he was being. "I...I just can't understand this." He shook his head as he laid her down. "It doesn't make any sense."

"Of course it doesn't." Rosie squeezed his arm. "Some things just don't. Let me get her changed. You go and make some coffee to warm her up."

Kenan backed slowly away from the bed, afraid to look away in case Catherine disappeared from view — and his life — again.

"Kenan!" Rosie waved her hand at him. "Give us some privacy."

He forced himself to turn and walk from the room, to drag his eyes away from Catherine's emerald green ones, though he longed to rush back to the bed and take hold of her — to shake her and force her to wake up properly, to explain where she'd been all this time when he'd been grieving her loss. Did she have any idea of how much he'd longed for her, missed her, worried about her?

He shut the door behind him and leaned his forehead against the solid wood, inhaling the comforting scent of the mountain pine. He would give Rosie a moment to help Catherine change and gather her wits but he needed some answers and he needed them tonight.

* * * *

"Here we are," Rosie announced as she returned to the room. "All dry and warm."

Kenan turned from where he'd been pacing in front of the fire. Matthew and Emmett had excused themselves from the house and gone out to tend to the animals in the barn. The storm had gathered pace and some of the beasts were becoming distressed. Ironic, Kenan had thought, as inside the house another storm was breaking.

Catherine emerged from behind Rosie and Kenan held his breath. He dug his fingernails into his palms to try to still their trembling. As she walked toward him, he glared at the vision who had haunted his day dreams, screamed for his help and protection in his nightmares and robbed him of all belief in his own masculinity. He had almost been destroyed by the realization that he hadn't been there for her. He hadn't protected her when she needed him most.

Damn it, she looked so good. Her hair glowed crimson in the firelight and in spite of his determination to remain aloof, his heart lifted at the sight of her even though his mind insisted that it was impossible. She'd been gone two years. Two whole years of missing that pretty face, those full sensual lips and that soft-as-velvet voice. Twenty four months of wondering how much she'd suffered, how long it had taken her to die and if she'd cried for him as she'd drawn her last breath.

If this was some kind of twisted dream he sure as hell didn't want to wake up. He'd had his fair share of those and waking always brought the fresh agony of renewed grief. Or relief in the case of the nightmares where her screams rang out and he was up to his knees in thick mud, unable to free himself, let alone her. He always woke from the nightmares in a cold sweat, his heart a wild mustang galloping and his own cries stuck in his throat. Once or twice—though he was ashamed to admit it—he'd even broken down and wept on waking, the sheer horror of his loss too much to bear.

This was actually happening and she was really at his homestead, walking toward him wearing one of his sister's old housedresses. Just like before. Like none of the bad things had ever happened and life was fine and dandy.

He shook himself. This would not do. He'd thought he'd never see her again, never converse with her or hold her close and it had drained him of everything he'd once been. Losing her had torn him apart and he'd had to adjust to giving up on the life he'd dreamt of. His days had become little more than just existing, as weak as an acorn calf.

Yet she was here.

She hadn't died. Hell, if this wasn't the opposite of an afterclap.

But images of the broken woman he'd imagined after her kidnapping resurfaced like flotsam on the sea, so he quickly snuffed his burgeoning hopes. He'd grieved for this woman once and no matter how she was here, how she'd survived, it would make no difference to him.

He had no intention of grieving for the titian-haired Catherine Montgomery a second time.

Catherine shook all over. Though this had been her intention all along, she couldn't believe that she was actually here, looking at Kenan once more. In the two years she'd been away, he'd matured and grown leaner. Yet he was even more desirable than she could remember. His hair was still thick and black, though there was a dusting of white at his temples as if age had tried to claim him but had lost the battle against youth. His jaw was still square, his mouth still full and his eyes...still so deep and dark. She had always been able to lose herself in his eyes.

But he looked shocked and furious and no wonder. He had probably just returned home after months on the Texas to Montana trail, expecting to rest up before heading out again. Instead, he'd been surprised by her arrival. How did she expect him to feel?

What a mess. She had never wanted it to turn out like this, never dreamt that it would. They'd had a good life mapped out, had been due to get wed and they had hoped to raise a family. It had been all she'd wanted, all he'd wanted. Their joy in each other had been so complete and intense that they'd neither wanted nor cared for anything else.

Even though she'd known that the life of a homesteader could be tough and harsh—especially for a woman— she'd still been happy to live that life, as long as it was with Kenan. The thought of their wedding had thrilled her and she'd even been excited about the *charivari*. Catherine had dreamt of how she'd keep their little farm in apple pie order and raise big strong boys to help Kenan out on the land and make him proud.

But after all that had happened, all the time that had passed, she doubted if there was any way to put it all right. Surely there was no way to ever recapture the innocence of their love. It would be like wading through quicksand—impossible and hopeless.

Catherine bit her lip. How awful to feel so estranged from the man she'd loved with all of her heart.

"We need to talk," Kenan gestured toward the table. "Sit."

Kenan lowered himself onto the bench at the rectangular pine table. He'd helped his pa make the long benches, but he wished they'd made them higher. At just over six feet tall, he had to sit with his knees almost pressing against his chest. He felt awkward and cumbersome, though he knew that his feelings had more to do with the new addition to his household than anything else.

He reached for his coffee and realized that he was shaking. Anger and grief boiled inside him and memories of the day he'd been told of Catherine's demise flashed before his eyes. He saw himself riding over to her uncle's homestead, jumping down from his horse, striding across the front porch, hovering his hand ready to knock...already aware that something was different, something was wrong. Usually, his arrival brought Catherine immediately to the door but this time she was nowhere to be seen.

Suddenly, her uncle had stood before him, eyes red, face blanched, a broken man.

"Kenan?" He was dragged back to the present.

"Huh?"

"Kenan?"

He jumped as the voice he'd believed he'd never hear again broke into his thoughts. She'd moved across the room like a spirit. For a moment his heated brain wondered if she was. Some folks believed that the spirits of the dead roamed the earth. Maybe she'd returned here to haunt him and she really was dead. The old familiar pain thudded though his skull like a tomahawk.

Catherine stood opposite him, hovering like a nervous bird beside the table.

"Sit down."

He gazed at her hand with its petite fingers and lightly freckled skin, as she placed it on the table. That hand belonged to the woman he had adored. He had showered it with kisses, held it over his heart when he proposed. She had gripped him with passionate ferocity when she had sought to pleasure him in return for the sensual delights he relished offering her. He hardened beneath the table as images of her encircling his erection and caressing the length of him before taking him between her breasts, flooded his mind.

"Kenan, are you okay?"

He shrugged, not meeting her eyes, not looking at her face. He couldn't. Instead, he drained the dregs of his coffee then stared into the bottom of the pewter cup, willing his cock to go down.

"Kenan?"

He tightened his hands around his drink.

"Kenan, please?"

The voice persisted, breaking into his consciousness, seeping into his soul like the warmth of the sun. It penetrated his tension, permeated his grief and reached down to his broken heart like a healing salve.

It carried him back to the summer they'd shared three years ago when she'd agreed to marry him. It had been the best summer of his life. He'd been helping her uncle with some work around his farm when Catherine had arrived, fresh from teaching college in the east. As her parents had both been taken by smallpox during her time at college, she'd had nowhere else to go than the home of her paternal uncle. She'd been delivered by wagon like an unwanted package one July morning. Kenan had watched her arrive. He'd been fascinated by her beauty in her green satin traveling attire, all wide eyes and fiery hair. His curiosity had been provoked and he had known at that moment, that she was the one for him, and that he'd do whatever it took to make her love him.

He slammed his cup on the table.

"What in the hell happened, Catherine?"

He glared at her.

"How are you here?" He gestured at her. "Alive?" His voice cracked on the final word.

He hung his head and ground his teeth. He would not submit to his grief and confusion. He was the man of the house, he had to be strong.

When he had reined in his emotions, he looked at her face. Her eyes glistened with tears like green pools freshly filled in a rainstorm.

"I'm so sorry, Kenan. I never wanted to hurt you."

He glanced around the room. Rosie was darning socks at the fireside now, attempting to give them some time to talk.

"Hurt me?" He frowned at the understatement.

"Well, yes…" She wrung her hands together on the table top. "I know that I've hurt you."

"You think that you hurt me, huh?" He sniffed. "Your uncle and aunt told me that you were dead, Catherine. Dead… Murdered by Indians, most likely the Sioux, on your way back from purchasing material for your wedding gown."

"For our wedding."

"But they lied."

"They did," she whispered. "It was wrong of them but please don't blame them…they had their reasons."

Kenan fought the urge to tell her exactly what he would do when he got hold of her uncle, reasons or not.

"So are you gonna explain? Or keep me hanging around for another two years so I can really feel the ache in my heart start to drain away my will to live?"

She stretched a trembling hand across the table toward him, the movement causing her sleeve to ride up her arm. He shivered as her cold fingertips met his skin and he swallowed hard to suppress the emotion rising in his throat.

Suddenly, he reached out and grabbed hold of her wrist.

"What in God's name is that?"

Chapter Two

Catherine tried to pull her arm away but Kenan's grip was too powerful. She struggled for a moment but he held on and the movement hurt. So, she gave in and slumped against the table. The wood was unforgiving beneath her breasts and she had to spread her legs to maintain her balance. Though she knew that the timing was wrong, she felt the flame of arousal flickering inside. The heat of Kenan's grip, the pressure against her hardening nipples and her open thighs, all combined to ignite her desire. She wished that she could clamber over the table top and cover his mouth with her own, push her tongue against his and run her hands through his thick, dark hair. It had been a long time since she'd felt such strong desire.

"What are these marks, Catherine?" He dragged her back to reality.

She tried to read his eyes—not so mad at her now but clearly confused.

She lifted her chin. "I burnt my arm on the stove."

"On the stove, huh? What" — he held her fast in one hand and ran the forefinger of the other over the scars — "ten, maybe twelve times?"

Heat filled her cheeks and she looked down at the table.

"Let me see the other arm."

She considered refusing but what would be the point?

He pushed up her sleeve and his touch made her jump as if a lightning bolt had struck her. Her heartbeat quickened and her body stirred like the creek bed when the first rains came. Kenan still roused her passion and though her mind screamed with fear at the idea of him discovering her secrets, her body responded to him, yearned for him, needed him. If only he'd gather her into his arms and press her against his chest, hold her close like he used to do.

"This one's worse, Catherine." He ran his finger over the red welts then gently released her, watching as she pulled her sleeves down. "What happened to you?" His tone was gentler now as if he sensed some of what she'd endured. But she couldn't tell him. She couldn't tell anyone. It was awful and she was ashamed.

"I was told that you were dead." He leaned forward and rested his elbows on the table. "Why would they lie unless...they had something to hide?"

She squirmed on the bench. He wasn't going to be fobbed off.

"Did someone hurt you?"

She bit her lip.

"Where did you go?"

Her stomach churned and she forced herself to meet his eyes.

"Catherine, if you're embarrassed...and your aunt and uncle were too...then you must have done something wrong." His words pierced her heart like an arrow.

He believed that she was to blame, just like her uncle had said he would.

"Did you run off with someone and your folks tried to hide their shame by telling me you was dead?"

The tears in her eyes brimmed over and trickled down her hot cheeks.

"That's it, isn't it?" he demanded. "You ran off with a man."

She watched helplessly as his anger took him farther away from her.

"You're nothing more than a harlot, Catherine Montgomery. You made me believe you loved me then you ran off with another man and your folks were so ashamed they had to make up some story about the Indians taking you."

She shook her head, the tears running down her chin and dripping onto her chest.

"Well explain it to me then." He stood, scraping the bench backwards as he did so.

"I can't," she choked out, hugging herself now as protection against his fury.

"I thought you were dead." His eyes were wide and wild. A lock of his dark hair tumbled over his forehead and she fought the urge to jump up and smooth it back.

Rosie appeared at Catherine's side and she rested her hands on the younger woman's shoulders.

"Kenan!" Her voice bore the assurance of the woman of the house. "This won't do any good. She's exhausted. Can't you see she's been through an ordeal?"

"An ordeal of her own making." He thumped the table with his fists. "I have grieved for you for two whole years, so smitten with you that I couldn't even look at another woman properly, let alone think of taking one to wife. No one could hold a candle to ya. It hurt so bad that even when I was full as a tick, I couldn't shake off your memory. And then you waltz back into my life, my home, my family…as if nothing ever happened."

He stepped over the bench and glared at her, making her heart lurch.

"Please, Kenan…" she proffered her shaking hands toward him. "Please don't be so mad at me."

"I want nothing to do with you. Nothing." He glared at her and when he spoke again his voice was dangerously low. "You can get yourself some rest for a few days but soon as you feel better, I want you out of here before anyone finds out. I'll not have people saying that the Duggans are the type of family to tolerate a harlot at their homestead."

Catherine watched, as powerless as a newborn foal, as he stormed off into the night, banging the door behind him. She sat still, frozen in time, listening carefully to the tearing of the seams at the edges of her composure. One by one, they unpicked until the grief came tumbling out and she hunched over her knees, surrendering to sobs that rendered her breathless. The guilt, the pain and the anguish came flooding out of her and she submitted to them all, no longer forced to suppress them.

Rosie rubbed her back and stroked her hair, then enveloped Catherine in her arms. The tender act brought more tears and Catherine cried until she was empty and her eyes were sore and swollen.

"He doesn't mean it, Catherine. He's just shocked to see you again is all. It's an enormous shock for him…for every one of us."

Catherine looked up and wiped her sleeve across her face.

"He'll never forgive me, Rosie."

Kenan's sister reached out and smoothed the hair from Catherine's face then took hold of her hands.

"Maybe not, Catherine, maybe not. Give him time and let him make up his own mind. But you'll have to be honest with him. A man and woman can't base a relationship on lies. You may never find the innocence of the love you had before but you may be able to salvage something. Even if it's just friendship. But you must tell him what really happened."

Catherine's eyes filled up again and she struggled against the choking pain in her throat. Tell him what really happened? That could never be. He was convinced that she was a harlot, that she'd willingly betrayed him. And in a way she had.

Kenan strode into the black night, oblivious to the rain that pelted his body, soaking him instantly and causing his clothing to cling to his skin. He walked right out of the gate and onto the path that led to the surrounding land then he began circling the perimeter fence. He took long strides, his pace increasing his heartbeat and forcing him to breathe quickly.

Darn it, he was so mad he was knocked galley west and he didn't know how in the hell he was going to recover. How could this have happened? He'd tried so hard to accept that Catherine was gone and now here she was, all pretty, sweet and vulnerable and he was likely to end up in a hoosegow if he didn't master his emotions.

He was horrified that she'd been hurt. Those marks on her arms had turned his stomach. He'd battled the anger within him since the day he'd been told of her disappearance and done his best to squash it down but every time a memory had surfaced or a nightmare had tortured him, he'd been all churned up again. Catherine had been the woman he was meant to protect, but he had failed.

Or he'd thought he had. Each time he'd followed what seemed to be a fresh lead in his continued search for her, it had come to a dead end and he'd finally been persuaded to give up. But he'd never stopped thinking about her.

Now it seemed that she'd actually made a choice and left him. Sure, she seemed ashamed of her scars but she'd been in no rush to explain them to him either. Maybe she'd gotten them leading some other fool into a false paradise.

So the grief he'd suffered had been an illusion and he'd been a fool. But now her jig was up and there was no way he was going to fall for her sweet deception again.

Catherine stood at the window and stared out into the darkness. Her head ached from crying but she was warmer now and the faint that had claimed her outside had passed. She'd walked all day without any food and the relief at arriving at the Duggan homestead had welled up in a swirl of emotion that had made her dizzy.

She could see her hazy reflection in the glass and she looked into her own eyes. Her pupils were so dilated that the green was barely visible and she felt that their ebony centers reflected the blackened hollow of her heart. She had done wrong and her soul was tarnished. Fear climbed up her spine like a dead man's fingers. What if the darkness kept on growing until it swallowed her whole?

She had loved Kenan and been devoted to him, but circumstances had taken her away from the path she had chosen. If she had felt that she'd had a choice then she would have followed that path unerringly, but she'd been torn apart and had made the only decision that she could have made at that time, as a young woman with people relying on her. She had owed her aunt and uncle her loyalty — they'd taken her in when she'd had no one else. It would have been wrong of her to abandon them when they had faced their own private troubles, but she wished that there had been another way.

Her lips trembled as she recalled of Kenan's words. He'd called her a harlot. The term churned in her gut and forced a sour taste into her mouth. She was no harlot, not really. She hadn't wanted to do what she'd done but sometimes life was unkind and it led her in directions she'd rather not have gone. Women didn't have as many choices as men in this world. Sure, things were improving and some women had even set up their own homesteads and businesses but it took courage, a strong will and self-belief.

Catherine hadn't needed to worry because she'd come fresh from college and the teaching examination to her uncle's farm where she'd met Kenan. Prior to college, which she'd been late attending because her Mama had needed her at home, she'd only wondered what it would be like to become a teacher. She had wanted to work with the children of the west before settling and having her own. Meeting Kenan had only confirmed to her that being a wife and mother was all she wanted in life. They would have carved out their path in the American landscape. It had been their mutual aim. How cruel it had been then when that simple dream had been stolen away.

A movement outside the window caught her eye and she leaned her forehead against the cold glass.

He was out there. He'd come back. She hurried over to the door and flung it open, ignoring Rosie's shouts and the fierce wind that whipped at her skirts as she ran out into the rain.

Kenan slumped against the gate, gazing into the darkness, fighting the urge to just lie down and be done with it all. He couldn't give up. He had responsibilities. But he felt so worn out, so much older than his thirty-two years. By now, a man should be wed and raising his children, not grieving daily and feeling so churned up all the time.

A noise startled him. He could just about make out a figure dashing toward him through the rain. It stopped in front of him on the other side of the gate.

"Catherine." Her white face was illuminated by the moonlight which peeped through the heavy clouds. She was a fallen angel. Her red hair clung to her cheeks and her cotton dress was like a second skin.

"Kenan." She held his gaze.

"You're getting drenched, Catherine. You'll catch cold and you've only just warmed up."

"I don't care, Kenan. I need to talk to you. To try to make you understand."

He shook his head. "I don't know that I can understand, Catherine." He couldn't let down his guard. She would just hurt him again and he couldn't afford that. The rain became heavier and way off in the distance, lightning pierced the sky.

"Please, Kenan." She reached out and touched his face, pressing the flat of her trembling palm against his cheek.

Her touch stirred him and he had to swallow hard against the pain in his throat. He covered her hand with his own and watched the spark ignite in her eyes. It brought a host of memories rushing back—times when he'd seen her eyes flash in that way when she was needy, passionate, eager. In spite of his doubts about her and in spite of his anger, another powerful feeling coursed through him. Desire. He desired her still. He desired her body, her touch and her fulfilment, which made his own all the sweeter. And he desired to lose himself, just for a moment, in order to escape the living hell he'd come to accept as normal.

"Come on." He opened the gate then walked through.

Thunder boomed like an angry cannon and large raindrops plopped into gathering puddles like tears from the heavens.

"Where?" she questioned and he could resist no longer. He leaned over and planted a kiss upon her luscious lips.

"Our old haunt."

He took her hand then headed toward the barn. She hurried to keep up with his large strides. As they approached, the door swung open and Matthew and Emmett emerged. *Darn it*. He'd forgotten they were out there. He pulled Catherine behind the oak tree that grew in the yard and placed a finger against her lips. The lightning illuminated the yard as it struck just feet away, causing Catherine to jump. Kenan covered her mouth with his hand and shook his head.

When his brothers had passed and gone into the house, he led Catherine into the barn.

He secured the door with the wooden bar. Then he turned to her. The dry warmth of the barn with its musky animal scent was comforting and it brought a wave of memories of times when he'd been here with Catherine before.

His heart beat so hard he felt like he would pass out. Excitement and fear coursed through his veins and he trembled with their effects.

As if echoing his inner turmoil, thunder cracked directly overhead. Catherine grabbed his shirtfront.

"It's okay," he whispered. "The storm will soon pass."

She leaned her head against his chest and he held her that way until her breathing and her trembling slowed. Droplets of water ran off the ends of her hair and soaked into his cotton shirt and he realized that she must be cold.

"I'll grab some of the blankets we keep for the horses. You'd better get out of your wet clothes."

She peered down at herself then back at him. In the darkness, the only illumination came from the intermittent flashes of lightning as they pierced small holes in the wooden walls, so he sensed, rather than saw, the uncertainty in her eyes.

"I…I don't know, Kenan."

"Catherine." He took her hand and squeezed it. "It's pitch black in here. I can't see a thing so I'm not going to be able to see you changing, am I?"

He held his breath as he waited for her response.

"Then light the lamp." She stood on her tiptoes and planted a kiss on his mouth. The cool featherlight touch of her lips against his sent fire through his body and he knew that he had to have her. He needed to feel her yielding beneath him, harlot or not. There was no going back as desire swirled like a hot fog through his mind and limbs, possessing him as he yearned to possess her.

He lifted the kerosene lamp from the peg by the door and lit it, then returned to Catherine's side. He watched the speedy rise and fall of her chest and wondered if it was due to fear or anticipation.

"Kenan?" Her voice fluttered over his skin like a butterfly's wings.

"Yes?"

"The blankets?"

He shook his head to clear the trance.

"Of course. Wait here." He pointed at her as if to hold her in place—as if to stop her from leaving his sight and his life again.

When he had retrieved two thick blankets from the tack room, he hurried back.

The center of the barn was empty. He lifted the lamp higher, creating a wider circle of light that reached the stalls, causing the beasts to stir. Catherine was gone. The circle of light shook and he turned around and around then rushed to the corners to check that she wasn't hiding. He'd known that it was too good to be true. Her presence must have been a figment of his imagination, a fever caused by being out in the storm. She really was dead, taken two years ago and he was alone. Grief, his familiar companion, began to swirl in his belly and sour bile filled his mouth.

"Kenan!"

An urgent voice from above caught his attention.

"What are you doing? I'm up here."

He raised the lamp and looked toward the trapdoor where a white oval face peered down.

"Come on up."

He rubbed his eyes. Of course she hadn't disappeared. He wasn't mad, hadn't invented her return. She'd merely climbed up to their own secret space where they'd spent many summer days and nights wrapped around each other, pleasuring their bodies in every way they could imagine. He grew hard at the memories and hurried toward the ladder.

Chapter Three

Catherine moved away from the trapdoor and crawled across the upper floor. When she reached the point where the ceiling was highest, she got to her feet and waited.

Just moments ago, as she'd looked down on Kenan, he'd appeared lost, his face blanched, his expression one of terror. She knew because she'd seen it upon her own face whenever she'd looked in the mirror during her time in New York. But why was he afraid? Did he believe that she had left him again? Her heart ached for all that he had suffered. For the things she'd put him through.

He had warmed to her during the course of the evening but she wondered how much. He needed her comfort, to be near her physically, and she could give him that much at least. Lord knew, she wanted it, too. But she doubted that she'd ever be able to mend him completely. She could see it now, even more clearly than before. He had loved her as much as she'd loved him and being separated from her had ripped him apart.

The light from the lamp reached the hatch then flooded the upper section of the barn. It threw shadows across the room, which increased her longing to be held in his strong arms. She wanted to feel safe again. She had dreamt of this reunion, yet never believed that it would really happen. She hadn't even known if she would make it back here or if he would be here if she did. The far off rumble of thunder brought a faint smile to her face. The storm had passed, for now. She leaned over and pulled off her wet, muddy boots, savoring the feel of the straw beneath her soles.

Kenan crawled toward her then stood. He had to hunch over, even at the roof's highest point and he looked so awkward. It reminded her of how he'd been when they'd first consummated their love. He'd been gentle, tentative, almost reverent in his perusal of her body. Though he'd not been totally innocent, he'd acted like a man making love for the first time and she'd appreciated it because she'd given him her virginity and wanted to feel that he was doing the same. He had admitted afterwards that he had lain with another woman but it had been different, not an act of real desire but a perfunctory act, a rite of passage.

"Why don't you sit?" She gestured toward the floor.

He put the lamp down then opened one of the blankets and flicked it out across the straw covered wooden boards. He lowered himself onto it and sat cross-legged, his hands on his knees.

Catherine summoned her courage. She would seize this moment and savor it. She might not get another chance. Kenan had been so angry with her earlier and she knew that once his tiredness cleared and his desire was spent, it could well return. Grief worked in strange, irrational patterns and she didn't want to give it the opportunity to claim him again just yet.

She pushed her wet hair over her shoulders and began unbuttoning the front of her housedress. She fumbled with the buttons because the wet material clung to them but the eagerness she saw in Kenan's eyes drove her on.

When she dropped her dress to the floor, he shifted his position and she could see the tell-tale bulge at his groin. She was exciting him and it thrilled her. She slipped down her petticoat and stood before him in her flimsy chemise, corset, bloomers and stockings. He was breathing heavily now and had shifted to his knees.

She froze.

"Please…keep going." His voice was husky with need. "Don't stop…"

"Of course not," she shook her head. She would not stop until she had eased his sorrow and hers. Temporary relief was better than none at all. They would live in the moment, be together for now.

She bent to peel off her stockings, but he pushed her hand away.

"Let me."

Catherine straightened up and stretched out a leg so that her foot rested upon his groin. She rubbed his crotch. He moaned and gripped her ankle, grinding against her toes.

When he slid his hands up her leg to her stocking top, it was her turn to gasp at the shivers his touch sent through her. Heat flickered between her legs. He peeled down the stocking then did the same with the other one.

"Nearly naked," he growled, as he slid his hands up to her waistband.

Her bloomers were stripped from her body in a flash and her corset soon followed. She had forgotten about this talent of his for removing clothing. His hands were skilled and dexterous. It amazed her that a man who was such an expert with a lasso and at delivering a trapped calf from its mother's womb could also be such a gentle yet masterful lover.

Kenan rose to his knees in front of her and pushed his face into the thin material that covered her stomach. She held him there, running her fingers through his thick hair and relaxing into his hands as he circled them over her back. He slid them lower then, to her buttocks where he squeezed and cupped her until she moaned with need. He pressed his fingertips between her buttocks and massaged toward her thighs, delving between her increasingly wet folds. She opened her legs and moved with his touch, eager to feel him inside.

When he pulled away, she bit her lip in frustration.

"Let me see all of you, Catherine."

She shrugged her drying chemise from her shoulders and allowed it to float down her body like a frothy white cloud to the floor. The air was cool as it met her skin but his hands were fire as he caressed her body.

"I missed you, Catherine." He stared at her, entranced, and she shivered under the intensity of his gaze.

"I missed you too, Kenan," she replied but swallowed the utterance, *though I doubt that you will ever really believe me.*

A frown passed across his face and she held her breath, afraid that she had ruined the moment, but it was quickly replaced with a look of desire and she let her breath out in a sigh.

He pushed his hands higher and she froze as he cupped her breasts. He fondled the heavy mounds and lifted them as if amazed at their weight.

"You have the most perfect tits, Catherine," he muttered, before covering them with hot kisses. "I have never seen their likeness."

Her heart sank as she realized that he had likely been with other women during her absence. She had hoped to keep him exclusively for herself but then she hadn't exactly been true to him. The disturbing images of faceless women were soon banished as he ran his calloused palms over her bosoms. It heightened her own longing and she surrendered to the need welling up within her. There would be time for worries and regrets tomorrow, but tonight was for pleasure and comfort. He suckled her nipples, rolling his hot tongue over each of them in turn, taking her eager flesh into his mouth. She could sense that his need was raw, that he wanted her as she did him.

"Touch me?" she asked.

"Of course."

His experience led him straight to the apex of her thighs where he rubbed and teased the soft rounded flesh of her legs. He brushed the back of his hands softly against the red curls at her groin and the gentle pressure made her bud swell in anticipation. She shivered as a knuckle grazed her clitoris making it tingle.

"Do you like that, sweetheart?" He leaned forward and kissed her navel, poking his tongue into the shallow hole. His hot breath fired her lust and she grabbed him by the hair then pushed her hips toward him to urge him to caress her fully. When his fingers parted the damp curls and met her silken folds, the sensation made her gasp. It had been so long since she had felt such tender cherishing. The summit of pleasure rose before her and she flung her head back and rode the waves that his delicate circling and massaging encouraged. Stars appeared then burst before her eyes, and she was catapulted through darkness then flung gasping into the light.

As her shuddering slowed, she loosened her grip on his hair. She had come so quickly under his knowing caress. It seemed that her longing for him had heightened her arousal, quickened her climax.

"You ready to ride a cowboy?" he asked. He slid a finger inside her, causing her to tremble with an aftershock of her climax then he added another, stretching her slightly, and she opened her legs to encourage him.

"Oh yes, Kenan…yes!" She gasped. The image of his thick hard cock filling her almost pushed her over the edge again.

When he withdrew his fingers she groaned with disappointment.

"Don't fret, Catherine." He chuckled. "I'll fill you up in due time."

He stripped off his clothing, and she eyed his lean, male body. His torso was golden from his time outdoors and his arms and shoulders rippled with his movements, displaying the well-honed muscles beneath the skin. His chest was broad, his stomach flat and his thighs large and muscular. And attracting her attention more than any other part of him, teasing her in the lamp light, was his thick, hard cock.

He lay back on the blanket and she realized that it was as if none of the bad things had ever happened. Things were as they had been and they would share their bodies, hearts and minds in this explosive union of man and woman. Their flesh would mold, their hearts would beat in time and they would become as one. They would know each other as only lovers could.

"Come here!" His voice was harsh with carnal thirst.

She lifted a leg across his body to straddle him then lowered slowly to perch upon his thighs. When she took hold of his erection he tensed. She gripped him in both hands, marveling at the sheer length and girth of him. He was a man amongst men and she had forgotten how magnificent he was.

She ran her hands up and down, stretching her fingers to circle his steel hard shaft. He moaned when she rubbed the thumb of her top hand over his tip to smear his thick juice. She licked her lips hungrily, aware that this fluid would ease his passage into her. As she fondled him, he lifted his hips and closed his eyes, giving into her hands and letting them guide him toward ecstasy.

She shifted down his body until her head was directly above his groin, then she lowered her mouth and flickered her tongue over the tip of his penis. His familiar taste filled her mouth and senses and she plunged him deep into her throat, yearning to join her flesh with his. Kenan cried out as she repeated the movement again and again and she felt his cock tensing and twitching against her lips and her tongue.

"Catherine, please." He suddenly stopped her. "I need you now. Be with me."

She needed no further encouragement. She lifted her head then shuffled forwards, pressing her labia onto him and guiding him toward her opening. He pushed against her and she sat upright, contracting her inner muscles to accentuate his sensation upon entry. He felt so big that she wondered for a moment if she could take him.

"You're so tight!" he exclaimed, gripping her hips and slipping into her inch by delicious inch, until she felt him stretching her inner walls, his bulging cockhead throbbing against her cervix.

"I've missed how you fill me, Kenan."

"I have missed your warmth around me, Catherine. And now I need to take you."

He began to move slowly in and out of her, gently at first so that he never left her completely. Each time their bodies met again, she felt the tingling in her sensitive bud increase. As their need grew, his thrusting increased in pace and he seemed to lose control. She cried out as he pounded relentlessly into her and sent waves of sharp sweetness cascading through her belly. It ached, yet it didn't, and she wanted him more and more.

The delicious sensations drove her onwards and she rode him fiercely, wildly, leaning her head backward so that her hair hung over his thighs. She pulled his hands up over her breasts, yearning to feel him squeezing them as she neared her climax.

"Catherine?"

"Please my love, don't stop!"

He obeyed and Catherine moved as one with him, their bodies united in a mutual goal. She had been thirsty as a woman lost in the desert but now she had found a mountain spring. Kenan was here, beneath her, and she was full of his cock, full of his need and full of pleasure.

They rolled over into the abyss together and she grasped at his hands, forcing his fingers to pinch her hard at her nipples. She bounced on him furiously, feeling his hot seed filling her depths and she kept moving until her climax slowed then faded away like a retreating thunder storm.

"I love you, Kenan," she spoke softly then raised his hands to her lips and showered them with kisses.

"I know," he replied. "I love you too.

As her own slick juices trickled down her thighs, mingling with his, she realized that he had just reopened her heart.

Chapter Four

Kenan awoke in the pale light of dawn and rolled over. He blinked hard as he stared at the beams above and tried to ascertain his whereabouts. Then it all came flooding back. He was in the hay loft. He'd come out here last night with Catherine and they'd experienced an explosive reunion.

He reached out for her, yearning for her warmth, but he found only the imprint of her body in the blanket covering the hay.

He sat up and looked around.

She was gone.

He leaned over and buried his face into the rough outline of her form. Her sweet fragrance made his breath catch in his throat. She had been here. It hadn't been a cruel dream. So where in the hell was she now?

He grabbed his clothes and crawled over to the ladder then hurried down to the barn.

A loud whistle when he reached the bottom rung stopped him in his tracks.

"Well whadda we got here?"

Kenan turned slowly, covering his groin with the bundle of clothing, to meet the smiling hazel eyes of his brother.

"Morning, Matthew." He offered a bashful grin.

"You been out here all night, brother?" Matthew frowned but Kenan could see that his lips were twitching at the corners.

"What of it?" Kenan dropped his clothes to the floor then began dressing.

"Nothing." Matthew grinned. "Nothing at all!"

"Have you...?" Kenan bit his lip.

"Have I seen Catherine?"

Kenan inclined his head.

"Sneaking into the house not half an hour ago, hoping to climb in beside Rosie before she notices." Matthew rubbed the nose of his mare as she poked her head over the gate of her stall.

Kenan pulled on his boots and hid a smile, imagining Rosie lying there feigning sleep whilst Catherine snuck into bed. At least he knew she'd been there with him all night. He'd slept so well, for the first time in two years, that he'd not even stirred when she'd risen.

"You know what you're doing, Kenan?" Matthew moved closer. "I mean..."

Kenan shook his head. "I really don't. It's just...I'm so...I wish I..." He held out his hands and shrugged. "It just felt so good to be with her again. I believed I'd never see her and I just wanted to hold her."

"I understand that, Kenan, I really do." Matthew squeezed his shoulder. "Did you manage to find out what happened to her? Where she's been all this time? She was in a bit of a mess last night." He looked down and scuffed the toe of his brown boot against the floor.

Kenan frowned. His empty stomach churned as the sense of calm he'd felt on knowing Catherine was really alive evaporated at Matthew's words. Matthew was right to question him. Last night, he hadn't found out where Catherine had been for the past two years. He'd become too emotional then got carried away on a wave of passion and need. He sighed.

"It's obvious she's been through something but when I asked her about it last night I got mad and she just clammed right up. It's gonna be hard to get her talking."

"Well, why don't you two take off somewhere today—get away from here and take her somewhere you used to go."

Kenan chewed his lower lip. It was a good idea. They wouldn't get much privacy if they stayed round the homestead and he couldn't leave things to simmer. Something was wrong and he had to know what it was, even if he didn't like it. The truth could be real tough on a man and he knew that if his suspicions about Catherine being with another man were right, it was going to tear him apart. But he had to know. Ignorance was worse. After all, hadn't he been ignorant of the fact that she'd actually been alive all this time? If he'd known she was still living he'd have continued hunting high and low for her. But he'd eventually given in and believed her uncle's tale.

Her uncle. He clenched his hands into fists. That man had allowed him to think that Catherine was dead, raped and scalped, buried in an unmarked grave or eaten by wild animals as her flesh had rotted quickly under the Montana sky. He had to get out to the old man's farm and speak to him, give him a piece of his mind, so that the old goat didn't think he'd gotten away with his deception.

"I'll get right on it, Matthew. Thanks!" Kenan smiled and ruffled his brother's hair then dodged out of reach. It was an old trick he used to remind his brothers that he was the eldest and could still show them a thing or two. Matthew laughed as he turned back to his horse, seemingly unaware that despite Kenan's jokey demeanor, his gut was churning and he was torn between dread and excitement at what the day held in store.

* * * *

Catherine held out her arms to Kenan and allowed him to lift her into the saddle then she swung her left leg over the horse. Matthew had been kind enough to let her take his mare so that she could ride out with Kenan. He'd told her that they were going out to check the surrounding land for possible expansion of their homestead but she knew better. The quick smile that had passed between Kenan and Matthew had told her enough. This trip was about her and Kenan having time alone.

Her stomach flipped. She wanted to be with him, more than she had ever wanted anything, but it also made her nervous. Last night had been wonderful but it had been a time for need and comfort. They had lost themselves in waves of passion and desire and become like wild animals intent upon reaching physical fulfilment. Today would be about honesty and confession and that concerned her. In Kenan's arms in the barn, she'd been able to pretend that all was well, to forget, even, what had been. But she knew Kenan and his solid belief in being forthright and just. His integrity held him firm like a solid stone pillar and it would crumble for no man or woman. There would be no more pleasure without pain.

She squinted against the bright sunlight and looked over at the house. Rosie stood in the window, her kind face pale and drawn. Catherine loved Kenan's twin dearly but she knew that Rosie's loyalty would always be first and foremost with Kenan. That was how it should be. She lifted a hand and smiled briefly, an attempt to reassure the woman who had once been her future sister-in-law. Rosie returned the wave then disappeared from sight.

"Shall we get going?" Kenan's deep voice broke her reverie and she turned to him and nodded.

"Rosie packed us a picnic." He tipped his hat forward to shield his eyes. "So we don't need to hurry back."

Catherine smiled but the lump in her throat stopped her from replying. It was going to be a long day.

* * * *

An hour later, Kenan led them through some trees and into a clearing alongside the fast flowing river. The recent rains had increased the volume of water and it now lapped crisp and clean against the banks. Kenan dismounted then helped Catherine down from the sturdy leather saddle. He held her against his chest for a moment and buried his face in her hair, savoring her sweet honeysuckle fragrance.

When he reluctantly released her, she sighed and smoothed out her skirts then walked a little way off and disappeared behind a tree. He swallowed the lump of insecurity that caught in his throat as he realized that she'd just gone to relieve herself.

He tethered the horses then gathered the picnic and blanket rolls from his saddle bags. In his haste that morning, he'd packed almost as much as he did to head off on the cattle trail. He just wanted things to be right.

"It's so beautiful here." Catherine's voice caressed him on her return to his side and he realized again how much he'd missed her.

Unable to reply, he laid out the blankets over the grass on the river bank. He straightened up and gazed at the panoramic Madison mountain range. The scenery was breathtaking. The flat grassy banks of the river curved slowly upwards as they spread out into the endless landscape, the green broken at intervals by gray stones and rocky outcrops. Far away in the distance, the jade tones darkened as they led up the mountain slopes and morphed into trees and bushes. The mountains themselves reached up into the sky, piercing the pure blue with their jagged ebony peaks. It made him feel insignificant, as if all that he did and experienced didn't really matter. It was both comforting and disquieting.

"Kenan?" He lowered his eyes from the vast Montana skies to meet those of the beauty beside him. "Shall we sit?"

"Yes." He replied. "For a while."

She lowered herself to the blanket gracefully and tucked her legs to the side then covered them with her skirts. He admired the elegance of her form, the straightness of her back and the way she held herself so ladylike. The churning began again in his belly as his pondered again about how someone could have hurt her and he balled his fists, feeling them trembling with the pressure.

"Are you okay?" She stared at his face, her green eyes full of concern.

He frowned. "Sure." His reply was cold and gruff. Of course he wasn't okay. What a ridiculous question!

Yet he should be okay, he had been reunited with the woman he loved. If only he could rid himself of the fear that now loomed like a dark cloud on his horizon, threatening to roll in like a thunderstorm and wash away his fragile hold on the joy he felt at her return.

"I need you to tell me everything that happened, Catherine."

"What do you mean?" Her voice shook and she glanced away, staring across the river.

"You know what I mean," he replied firmly.

"But today was about us having some time to..." She paused and licked her lips before looking at him. "Time to be alone."

"Dammit, Catherine! Of course I want time alone with you but the questions I have are eating me up inside. I need to know what happened when you were away...hell, even why you went away and left me grieving. I'd never have put you through that!"

"I didn't want to, Kenan, I swear it!" Her eyes glistened with tears and he fought the urge to reach out and pull her to him. "I had no choice. Please believe me."

"Then start explaining." He pushed his Stetson back on his head then smoothed away the beads of perspiration on his brow. "Prove it."

She took a deep breath then exhaled shakily. "Okay. But you have to be patient with me and promise not to get angry. Can you do that?"

He scowled. He couldn't promise not to get angry—he was already like a pot beginning to simmer—but he would try to contain that anger until he'd heard her out. He had to...for both their sakes.

Chapter Five

Catherine arranged her skirts around her modestly and took a deep breath. She had to do this. She knew that she owed it to Kenan but also knew that it would be extremely difficult.

She stared into his cocoa brown eyes and marveled at how they reflected the beauty of the surrounding landscape. It was as if he had absorbed the scenery — from the high ebony peaks of the mountains to the cool rushing depths of the river — and become one with it. He was strong and brave, kind and compassionate and Catherine was afraid that she would destroy him with her confession. She wanted to lean across the blanket to kiss him, to shower his handsome face with a display of her love. It was a battle to deny her basic urges. Not yet, not now.

"Kenan?"

He inclined his head then crossed his legs in front of him, getting comfortable to listen to her story or bracing himself for unpleasant revelations.

"This is very hard... I'm not sure where to...oh, I don't know where to start." She wrung her hands in her lap.

"The day you disappeared," he spoke softly. "Start there."

"Of course." She sighed, relief washing over her at his calm tone. "My uncle had packed the wagon with some produce which he aimed to sell in Virginia City. I went along for the ride because he suggested that I could pick out some material for my wedding gown."

"You know I'd have married you in your regular old housedress, don't you?"

The dark shadows beneath his eyes made him appear older than his thirty-two years.

"I do, Kenan. But I wanted something pretty. I wanted to look special for you."

He pulled a blade of grass from the ground and ran it through his fingers. She watched the movement, welcoming the momentary distraction.

"So I went in with him. My aunt stayed on at the farm. She claimed to have a headache. I offered to remain with her but she burst into tears and shut herself up in her room. I was under the impression that it must be her..." Her cheeks flooded with warmth. "Her monthlies, so I left her to it. I now know that she was distressed at what was about to happen."

Kenan frowned. "So she knew that you wouldn't return?"

"She was near hysterical. She always had an inclination toward the dramatic." She gave a wry smile, recalling several times when her aunt had demonstrated mood swings an actor would envy. "But that day, she seemed different."

"But she still let you go?" He shook his head.

"As we drove away, I spotted her at the bedroom window. She held a hand over her heart and mouthed that she loved me."

Kenan threw the blade of grass away and rubbed his hands on his trouser legs.

"Love?" he huffed.

"I think she did in her own way. But this was bigger than her...more than she could handle." Catherine held her hands apart in front of her to illustrate her point.

"So what happened when you got into town?"

"We dropped off the supplies then my uncle said he had business at the saloon."

"The saloon?"

"Yes." She picked at a nail. "He had to meet someone there."

"But he didn't..." He scowled.

"No, he didn't take me in. I waited outside in the wagon."

Catherine's stomach churned as she recalled waiting outside the noisy, smoky saloon. She'd had a feeling that something wasn't right, that her uncle was up to something but no idea what. She'd even pitied the whores that had spilled out onto the muddy street, their thin bodies covered only by soiled undergarments and bruises. One had glared at Catherine and eyed her traveling attire as if she'd rip it from her frame out of sheer jealousy and bitterness. If only she'd known that a similar fate had awaited her too.

Kenan adjusted his position then reached out, gently fingering the hem of her gown. He smoothed it down against the blanket and the innocent gesture increased her heartbeat. She still loved him so much and her heart ached for all that he'd been through.

"After a while…I'm not sure how long, but it must have been more than an hour, my uncle emerged, squinting against the midday sun. He'd clearly been drinking and he stumbled as he walked toward the wagon. That was when I started to feel afraid."

Kenan moved closer to her and he took hold of her right hand in both of his.

"Go on."

"He told me to get out of the wagon. So I did. I was confused but I hoped that maybe he just needed my help getting in as he had consumed a fair amount of whiskey."

She looked at Kenan, but he stared off into the distance. A muscle in his cheek twitched, reminding her of an angry cat's tail.

"He took me by the hand and dragged me toward the saloon. By this time I felt sick. I begged him to stop, told him that he would ruin me by taking me into such a place but he seemed oblivious to my concerns." Kenan squeezed her hand and she ran her thumb over his fingers. "As we burst through the doors, it seemed that everything went silent. It was so…so dark inside and so smoky. The stench of stale liquor made me nauseous. I could barely see." She bit her lip as tears threatened to fall.

"Then what?" Kenan uttered through clenched teeth.

"He led me toward the back of the place and into a small room where three men sat around a table playing cards."

"I cannot believe that he did that to you!" Kenan growled. "He knew that we were to be wed yet he took you into a saloon, in broad daylight…my fiancée!"

Catherine felt the sting of tears and her throat tightened. She had known that Kenan would be angry and she had only just begun to explain. She choked out, "I'm so sorry!"

"No, no, sweetheart." He leaned over and pulled her onto his lap. She relaxed into his strength, allowing him to comfort her though she felt that she did not deserve it. "It wasn't your fault. Your uncle was in the wrong and I shall have words with him about this."

"No!" she squeaked. "Please, no. It's not what I want."

He pulled her against his chest and kissed her forehead. "It seems that your uncle showed little concern for what *you* wanted, Catherine."

She sniffed then took the handkerchief that he offered. "I know...but it was so difficult for him."

"Please don't try to excuse him any further, Catherine, because I cannot promise to remain calm." Kenan's voice was tight with control. "Now, please continue. Who were the men?"

"I'm not sure about two of them but the one that worried me was clearly the wealthiest. I could tell from his clothing—it was of the fashionable New York style. He was a large man, hefty as a bull with hair the color of dirty straw combed across the dome of his head and"—she shuddered as the memories flooded in—"he looked at me as if I were a mare for sale."

She felt Kenan stiffen at her words but he said nothing.

"My uncle stood me in front of him and removed my shawl then he told me to turn around. I would have started crying but I felt furious that I was being treated in this way. I had no idea what my uncle was doing. I refused." She lifted her chin in remembered indignation.

"So what did they do?"

She gazed at the cool river bubbling past them. How nice it would be to throw herself into the frothy surge and be cleansed of all that had happened, all that she had done. But no water could wash her sins away.

"They laughed and the wealthy man said that I would do."

"Do for what?"

Catherine sighed then brought Kenan's hand to her lips and kissed it. "I would do for what my uncle owed him."

She felt Kenan's fingers bite into her upper arms as he pushed her away from his chest to look at her. "William Montgomery sold you?" His eyes were wide.

"Not exactly sold me..." She paused, searching for the right words but there were none.

"Then what? It sounds like he passed you on like a soiled dove to the highest bidder!"

"No!" She reached out and placed a trembling hand upon his chest. "He didn't sell me. He just... He gave me a choice."

"Doesn't sound like that to me, Catherine!" The fury in Kenan's eyes frightened her. This was why she had gone along with it at the time. She had known that if she had tried to say goodbye that he'd have gone after her uncle, gone after them all.

"My uncle asked to have a quiet word with me and the man agreed. He said we had twenty minutes then he wanted an answer or he'd be claiming his winnings. So we went outside and Uncle William tried to explain."

"I cannot see what explanation would justify what he did!" Kenan spat. He slid Catherine off his lap and stood up. "I'm sorry. I'm finding this hard to take!"

"Of course," she whispered. "I knew you would. Why don't we take a break? Maybe"—she looked at the water—"find a spot where we can swim?"

He turned eyes full of gratitude toward her. "Yes. Let's take a break. Then you can tell me the rest."

He took her hand and helped her to her feet then led her past the horses and through the swishing trees and the pale lemon faces of the flowers turned eagerly toward the sun. She followed him gladly, as she had always known that she would.

Kenan stopped at a point where the bank grew flatter and the grass gave way to silt and sand. The water was shallow and crystal clear over the stones and Catherine suddenly realized how hot and uncomfortable she felt. High summer in Montana was usually hot and uncomfortable but this year it seemed hotter than hell. Beads of perspiration trickled down between her bosoms and the backs of her knees were clammy beneath her stockings.

"Let's go in. It looks wonderful!"

Kenan smiled at her.

"You always loved to swim, Catherine."

They removed their shoes and outer garments then stood awkwardly.

"What now?" he asked.

"Just like always!" She chuckled.

His fingers trembled as he unhooked the front of her corset. He let it drop to the ground on top of her dress, then moved closer to her and encircled her wrist with his hands.

Her stomach flipped at the passion she saw in his gaze. He wanted her and loved her still but she had not yet revealed all to him. When she did, she feared that he would cast her aside like a broken saddle or a worn out boot.

"Hey!" He tipped up her chin with a fingertip. "What is it?"

She shook her head. "Nothing, just memories."

"Good ones I hope." He sighed as he bent his head to kiss her.

At first the kiss was soft and she relaxed into the warmth of his mouth, the sweetness of his breath. But as he pushed his hot tongue between her lips, she moaned and slid her hands through his hair. She filled her palms and her fingers with it then pulled his head toward her.

As they kissed, he loosened the waistband of her bloomers and she felt them slide down to the floor. The warm afternoon air caressed the naked skin of her legs and fluttered the edge of her chemise. Kenan held her body against the length of his and she felt his erection rock hard against her belly. She giggled.

"What is it?" he asked breathlessly.

"Perhaps we'd better cool off?"

He looked down at the large bulge at his groin. "Maybe."

He shrugged out of his union suit sleeves then slid it down over his legs.

Catherine swallowed hard as she stared at his body. The hard cock stood to attention, pointing outwards from the dark curls of his pubic hair and pulling her eyes toward the balls beneath. He was a perfect male and she yearned to become one with him, to take him deep inside her and ride him until they both reached the point of no return.

"Now you!" His voice was husky but his tone was firm.

She undid the button at the front of her chemise then lifted it over her head. It was sheer as gossamer and featherlight. When she met his eyes again, the intensity of his gaze startled her. He looked so fierce, like he was about to explode with need and desire.

He took her hand and led her toward the water's edge.

The cool river lapped at her toes and her nipples hardened, making her full breasts tingle. "It's freezing!"

"You'll get used to it!" He eyed her naked form.

He waded into the water until it reached his thighs then turned to face her. Catherine watched as goosebumps rose on his arms and the neat sack of skin that held the essence of his masculinity pulled itself up toward his body.

But his erection still stood firm and ready, the tip shimmering with a diamond like bead of moisture.

In a flurry of excitement, she pulled the pins from her hair and let its vermillion waves cascade down her back. The breeze lifted it and swirled it around her face, teasing her by limiting her view of Kenan. She flicked her head to push it aside and fixed her eyes upon the man she loved.

Unable to resist any longer, she ran to him, splashing the icy water over them both as she did so. The river's chilly grip traveled quickly up her legs and the tiny hairs on her neck and her arms stood on end. Kenan grabbed her and pulled her with him into the flow and Catherine gasped as the cold water enveloped her, touching her inside and out. The sensation of the chilly water delving between the hot sensitive folds of her most private place was delicious and it heightened her desire to feel her lover's cock there too.

"It's freezing, Kenan!" She giggled.

He laughed then flicked water into her face. She shook her head, her thick hair heavy with the river. He reached out and tenderly spread her hair out so that it floated around her like a gathering of eels come to inspect her nudity.

"Come here!" Kenan embraced her. Their cold, wet skin and his solid length prodding into her stomach fired her yearning to have him. She wanted to possess this man once more, before he knew the full truth. The fear that he might abandon her when she confessed all darkened her mind for an instant, like a cloud passing over the sun. But she shrugged it away, refusing to allow it to spoil this precious moment.

Kenan pushed her toward the bank where he laid her on her back in the shallows. He eyed every inch of her body. The stones and sand were hard and cold beneath her skin but the fire in his gaze warmed her like the hot summer sun. He stroked his hands over her stomach, across the curves of her hips then back toward the apex of her thighs. She moaned as he parted her legs and ran the fingers of his right hand between her swollen lips then over her aching bud. He rubbed it between his thumb and forefinger with a touch so experienced and knowledgeable that Catherine felt all sense and reason slipping away. Lost in passion, she lifted her hips toward him, eager for him to fill her up as she knew only he could.

Whilst he massaged her, he used his free hand to drip chilly droplets of water over her burning cunny. She flung out her arms and grabbed his shoulders, digging her nails wantonly into his flesh and pulling him down onto her, unable to wait another second. His body molded to hers as if it were the other half of her and she flung her head back as he drove his erection into her soft flesh. As excitement consumed him, he rocked into her, harder and faster and she spread her legs farther to take him deeper. The water splashed around them as they moved in perfect union and the current flowed over them, caressing their skin and creeping into forbidden places as if to join in their lovemaking.

Catherine bit into Kenan's shoulder when the tensing and twitching of her pussy signaled the onset of her climax and her sensitive bud throbbed then burst into countless little explosions like lightning bolts piercing the night sky. The aftershocks flooded throughout her entire body and her hot juices flowed from her loins. Her excitement spurred Kenan on and he thrust harder and faster before freezing as he reached his own shuddering release.

He rested his weight on his elbows and looked into her eyes.

"You are amazing," he whispered as he gently pushed the wet hair from her forehead. "No one should ever hurt you. Ever."

"Kenan?" Her eyes filled with tears as the realization that she still might make him hate her flooded back like the chill of the water that now seeped between their heated bodies, teasing his ejaculation away from her in the same way that she feared her confession would drive him away.

"Not yet." He eased himself out of her then helped her to her feet. "Let's dry off."

When they were wrapped up in the blankets and she sat between his legs, leaning against him, she tried again.

"Shall I continue?"

"Okay." His reply was barely audible and she sensed his reluctance. Now that they had rediscovered each other, neither wanted to feel any distance between them again, but they both knew that she had to speak and he had to listen. They had to have honesty even if they had nothing else.

"Where was I?" she questioned.

"Your uncle took you outside the saloon to explain what he needed from you."

Her heart ached to hear the bitterness which had returned to his tone and she steeled herself as she prepared to break his heart all over again.

Chapter Six

Kenan pulled the blanket tighter around his shoulders and buried his face in Catherine's hair. It was damp and smelled of the river, earthy yet fresh, and it stirred something primitive within him. He wanted to protect this woman, to offer her everything that he had but he had to know what had happened to her so that he could help her to heal—help them both to heal.

Catherine shivered suddenly and Kenan pulled her closer. All that separated them was the blanket wrapped around her and though he knew that he had to focus on what she was about to tell him, his cock twitched with excitement at her proximity. He willed it to stay down, knowing that having his erection digging into her back would not help her to relate what she had been through over the past two years.

"So my uncle took me outside the saloon." Her voice was soft, her tone cautious.

"And what did he say?" Kenan tried to sound neutral.

"He told me that the man in the saloon had offered him a deal."

"For what?"

"My uncle had been gambling...for quite some time...and had gotten himself into a lot of debt."

"What a wasteful scoundrel! How damned irresponsible can a man be when he's got two women dependent on him for bed and board and—"

"Kenan!" Her voice cracked on his name. "It happened. We can't change it no matter how angry we might feel."

He hung his head, resting his chin in her hair. "I'm sorry. I know that."

"The man in the saloon had lent him money and now he wanted it back. With interest."

"He could have sold the farm."

"It wasn't enough," she whispered.

"What?" Kenan pulled away from her and moved around so that he could look at her. The blanket slipped from his shoulders and dropped to his waist but his anger was making him hot and he was glad to be free of it. "How much did he owe?"

"He didn't tell me exactly." She pulled her knees up to her chest and hugged them. "But it was more than he could repay."

His heart ached as he looked at her. With her face fresh and glowing from the river and their lovemaking and her hair wet and dark with water, she looked so young and innocent. Her eyelashes were still thick with moisture and they clung together, framing her emerald eyes. Surely any man who knew this woman would want to serve and protect her, not force her into the life of a whore. What in hell had her uncle been thinking? Damn it! Kenan knew that he'd have sold his homestead, his animals, even the hair on his head to keep that from happening. If only she'd come to him, let him know, asked for his help!

"God damn!" Kenan spat. "I tell you Catherine, I know you said that you don't want me to speak to him but this is just unforgiveable. How the hell did he get himself into such a mess?"

She shrugged. "My aunt was a fine looking woman in her youth. I think he went all out to get her then to keep her and it just spiraled out of control. When he couldn't give her the child she craved, he developed a taste for drink and for gambling and…he just lost control."

"But to sell his own flesh and blood."

"He didn't sell me!" Her voice trembled and his heart ached to see her try to hold on to some pride with the tilt of her chin. "I offered."

"You offered?" He frowned, the churning beginning afresh in his gut. "You…offered to leave me…to give yourself to…" He spat on the ground. "You went with that man voluntarily?"

She raised tear-filled eyes to meet his. "I knew that it was what my uncle wanted…needed! They were going to lose everything. He wasn't well and they weren't getting any younger. They took me in…"

Kenan reached out and took her hand. "We could have found another way to help them. You didn't have to do that."

"You don't understand. He…the man…he told my uncle that I had to decide then and there. He said that if I chose not to go with him that he would take all that he was owed immediately. I was put on the spot. I had no choice. What if you'd been too furious to help them out…what if…?"

"Did you not know me at all?" He jumped to his feet, the blanket falling to the ground. "I loved you so much I'd have done anything for you, Catherine! Anything! It breaks my heart that you...that you doubted me."

She shook her head. "I didn't doubt you. I just faltered, just for a moment was all. And all I had was a moment to decide, Kenan. Please understand me."

He stood in front of her, the breeze caressing his skin where just moments ago she had been pressed against him. His nipples tightened and goosebumps rose on his naked flesh. His balls pulled toward his body and he became suddenly aware that his cock was swinging free, still moist with their combined fluids, as exposed to the elements as his heart now was. He crouched down and pulled the blanket around his waist.

"I'm trying to understand, Catherine, I promise." He took her hand again. "Please, continue."

"So I offered and he burst into tears, said I'd saved his skin and he'd always be grateful. Then he said we'd have to go back into the saloon and let the man know."

Kenan ground his teeth together. William Montgomery had clearly been a chicken shit son of a bitch who'd exploited his beautiful niece to save his own skin. Kenan had no intention of letting the old man get away with his crimes.

"When we returned to the saloon, we were directed to a room out the back. I was so afraid that I could barely put one foot in front of the other. My uncle had to guide me through the bar to the room at the back, drunk as he was."

"I swear, Catherine, I'll..." Kenan choked down his angry words. What good would it do to let it all out? He needed to listen, then he'd decide what action to take.

"He knocked on the heavy door then pushed me forwards and I swear I nearly swooned when we walked in. The man sat on a red mahogany couch, puffing on a fat cigar. When we entered he grinned like a hungry mountain lion that's just seen a fattened calf. I would've turned and run if I'd not had my uncle's hand in the small of my back."

Kenan squeezed her hand and felt the small bones shift beneath his fingers. "I wish I'd been there to protect you, Catherine. I should have been there."

"You couldn't have been with me all the time, Kenan. What happened...it was wrong and it wasn't fair and sometimes I'm so darned mad about it myself that I could scream for hours but it wouldn't help anything. It wouldn't change anything."

He swallowed hard to try to dislodge the lump in his throat. She had been through so much and yet she was still so brave, so stalwart. No wonder he loved her so much. She'd make any man proud to call her wife.

"The man introduced himself."

"What was his name?" Kenan growled.

"If I tell you, Kenan, you must promise me not to go after him."

He shook his head. "I just...I can't..."

"Then I can't tell you."

"No...tell me, please. I just need to hear his name."

"Thomas Henderson."

"Of the shipping family?"

"Yes."

So the filthy rich son of a New York shipping merchant had waltzed into town and taken away his fiancée—probably just for the fun of it. Men like that toyed with young women like a cat would play with a mouse, then cast them aside when they were too broken and jaded to be fun anymore.

"He told my uncle to take a seat opposite then he motioned for me to sit at his side. My legs were trembling so darned much I near fell onto the sofa. He asked me if I knew what he wanted, so I replied that I knew that my uncle was in debt and that apparently I could pay off that debt."

"And?"

"Henderson explained the terms." She rested her forehead on her knees. "He said that my uncle's debt was so great that it would take quite some time to pay it off. If I was serious about helping...I had to know what was involved."

"The filthy bastard! I'll hang him from the nearest tree if I ever get my hands on him. I swear I'll—"

"No!" Her retort was cold and firm. "It won't do, Kenan. I went along with it and now the debt is settled. I won't have retribution and the grief that it will cause. Can't you see that I did what I had to and now I'm back? I have to move on or else I'd just as well give up! I didn't go through all that...all those days and nights of...of suffering...just to throw everything away!"

Her eyes filled with tears and her lower lip trembled.

"I might be wrong but you seem to have feelings for me still." She blinked hard. "And maybe we can salvage something from this mess but not...not if you're intent upon revenge. Thomas Henderson is a rich and powerful man and if you go up against him, Kenan, you can only lose. And I agreed remember...no one forced me!"

Kenan ground his fists into his eyes and tried to calm his breathing. What Catherine said made sense even though it wasn't what he wanted to hear. Another man had taken the woman he loved as payment for a debt incurred by her uncle. It was outrageous, disgusting and immoral but she had gone along with it. The law was hard to implement at the best of times and Henderson was a man with means, with power. In comparison, Kenan was a cattle driver with a small homestead. He did all right but he'd be no match for the likes of Henderson...not if he went about it the legal route anyhow.

"Okay, Catherine," he whispered. "I'll put all desire for retribution aside." *For now*, he added to himself. "Please just finish explaining."

"He took my hand and I had to fight the urge to snatch it back. The smoke from his cigar burnt my eyes and made me want to cough. But I couldn't take my eyes off his face, Kenan! It was huge! Like a large florid sack broken only by his beady gray eyes which reminded me of small rocks stuck in a mud pie. I later found out that he was only in his early thirties—same as you—but he looked much older 'cos of the bright red veins running from the sides of his nose like cracks in the scorched earth." She shuddered and Kenan ground his teeth together at the image she'd created.

"He said that I was an attractive woman and that with the right clothes and perfumes I could make a man real happy."

"What a blowhard!"

"I guess I looked kinda country-girl compared with the fine New York ladies." She looked up from beneath her lashes.

Kenan eyed her thick red curls, her pretty little nose with its spattering of freckles then into her bright green eyes. There was nothing about her that any woman — wealthy and spoiled, fine and aristocratic — could ever top in his eyes. Catherine was perfect, beautiful, bright and sweet. And she had been his woman, his world, his future.

"He asked if I'd be prepared to try to make him happy. Though it made me feel sick, I said that I'd do whatever was required of me for however long it took to pay off the debt. I was hoping that he'd say a week or two, a month at most, so when he said two years I nearly vomited all over him."

"That's why you've been gone so long."

"Yes...He said they'd deal with matters in Virginia City by telling folks I'd been taken by Indians. They'd make it look like I'd been kidnapped and my uncle would spread the story."

"By 'folks' he meant me."

"Mainly. My uncle had told him I had an intended."

"And that didn't bother him?"

"He asked me straight up then if I was intact."

"What?" Kenan had to force his mouth shut. "What did you say?"

"I told him the truth. I didn't want to lie in case it made the deal null and void. He said it didn't bother him and made a comment about it making the way easier for him." Her face drained of all color at the memory.

"Oh, Catherine!" Kenan's blood boiled as the meaning behind her words sank in. The man had fully intended to keep her as a whore — to use her perfect body, to delve into her bright and inquisitive mind, to take from her what was a gift for her to bestow upon the man she loved.

"Then he pulled a paper from his pocket. He said that I had to sign it to make the contract real. My uncle's bleary eyes were on me and I could read the desperation in them. So I did it. Though my heart thrummed like a trapped butterfly and my stomach felt like it would empty its contents right then and there, I signed away my life for two years…and became…" Her eyes brimmed with tears. "I became a harlot!"

"Oh my sweetheart." Kenan moved closer to her and stroked her cheek with the back of his hand, smoothing away the tears as they burst forth and ran like raindrops down her flawless cheeks.

"He took me to New York City where he kept me in a set of rooms in a large fancy house like some kind of pet bird. For a while, he kept me hidden away, to let things blow over here, he said. But after about two months, I'm not sure exactly 'cos I didn't have any way of keeping track of time, he started taking me out to the theater and to dine with his acquaintances."

"During which time I was grieving for you, thinking you'd been killed and scalped and…ra…" Kenan choked on the last word.

"I'm so sorry."

"Me too." He sniffed, fighting against his own tears of anger and frustration.

"If I could have seen another way, Kenan, I would have taken it."

He shook his head. What did it matter now?

"Did he hurt you?"

She sighed. "Do I have to answer that?"

"I need to know, Catherine or it will haunt me forever."

"He used me as a man would his wife. He wasn't exactly tender but he didn't, ya know, hurt me down there." Her cheeks filled with color and she hung her head. "He knew I was no virgin so there were no coy games. I don't want to…I can't describe the details so

please don't ask me to. Those I really need to forget."
She chewed her lip. "But, no, he didn't hurt me in that
way."

"I cannot bear to think of you…" Kenan took a deep
breath, swallowing the words that would only cause
her pain and shame. She was embarrassed enough
and had suffered enough.

"Kenan." She let the blanket fall to her waist and he
gasped at her exposed beauty. Her hair tumbled all
around her, curling as it dried, its titian waves
reminding him of the flame colored streaks painting
the sky in a beautiful sunset. The milky skin of her
neck and torso were soft and unblemished, broken
only by the large rosy circles at the center of her full
heavy bosoms and the hard pink nubs that begged to
be touched and taken deep into his hungry mouth.

He watched, spellbound, as she placed a quivering
hand over her heart. "I swear to you that although I
submitted my body, I never surrendered my heart or
my mind. And…though it'll not be of much
comfort…you should know that the attentions he paid
me did not last long. When he realized that he was
unable to penetrate my coldness, unable to sever me
from my loyalty to you, he seemed to lose his
virility… In fact, he lost the urge to even try. My scorn
emasculated him and he was unable to—"

"It's okay!" Kenan stopped her. "Pray do not say
anymore, you do not need to."

"I'm so sorry to upset you. I'm so ashamed, Kenan."

"It's not you who should be ashamed, Catherine. So
how…did you get the marks on your arms?" As he
asked the question, he ran a fingertip over the red
welts that marred the ivory skin.

"Those are the markers to show the passing of time.
He said I was like a bonded slave, that I would be his

for two years and that he would mark me for every month that passed so that I would know how long I had left."

"How did he…?"

"With a red hot knife sharpened by his manservant. Henderson would heat it until it smoked then press it into my skin, dragging the blade through the flesh." Her eyes glazed over as she spoke.

"The crazy bastard!" Kenan cursed. "He had no right to do this! No right at all!"

"It was strange but in a way I almost welcomed the pain. It distracted me from the hurt inside and felt like a physical manifestation of it, plus each burn brought my freedom closer."

"If only I'd known you were alive! I'd have come for you. I'd have torn him apart with my bare hands. Why didn't you get word to me?"

"I knew that you would do that and also that it would solve nothing. Violence would have led to more violence. I had to hope that you loved me enough to keep going—to keep the memory of our love alive. I couldn't risk you coming to New York and ending up dead. He'd have destroyed you way before you got to him. He was so powerful, so connected. I knew that I had to wait it out…to play his game."

"Kind of a sick game, don't you think?"

"It was. I know. But…There was a get out clause."

Kenan raised his eyebrows.

"He said that if I fell in love with him…then he would stop marking me and if I could submit my heart and mind to him as I did my body then he would make me a free woman."

"I don't understand. You mean…if you'd just told him that you loved him he'd have let you go?"

"But I couldn't, Kenan."

"Why not? You could have come home to me sooner! Got word to me that you were safe."

She shook her head. "The only thing that kept me sane all that time as I serviced him and paid off my uncle's debt was knowing that although he'd taken my body, although he'd treated me like I was no better than a painted cat, he would never, ever possess me like you had. You have to understand that I absolutely could not give him anything else. He had my physical being and could command my presence whenever he chose but he would never ever have my love. That has...and always will remain...only yours."

"Catherine!"

He pulled her toward him and into his arms, devouring her with kisses that told of his own undying devotion and at first she remained stiff, rigid with the pain of her memories but as he continued to kiss and caress her, he felt her melt in his arms, surrendering to his embrace and to her love for him.

* * * *

Catherine smoothed out her skirts then held her arms out to Kenan. He lifted her up to the saddle as easily as if she were a small child. She cocked a leg over the horse and slipped her foot into the stirrup. A tingling between her legs made her smile and she shifted slightly to adjust the material of her drawers.

"What's funny?" Kenan looked up at her as he tightened the saddle then secured her foot in the stirrup.

"Our lovemaking has left me a little..." Her cheeks filled with heat. "Tender and, dare I say it, damp!"

He laughed then ran a hand up under her skirt, caressing the smooth skin of her thigh until he could cup the side of her buttock that was not touching the saddle.

"Wet and tender. We'd better get going or I will have to pull you down from the saddle and take you again!"

Catherine gasped. Following her confession, he had taken her into his arms and made love to her again, kissing every inch of her skin with a tenderness and passion that had brought tears to her eyes. He had even kissed every one of her scars and told her that they would always be reminders of how he had once lost her and how brave she had been.

Catherine was amazed at his understanding. She had feared losing him forever after she told him of her time as a bonded whore but he seemed accepting, if not unperturbed. How could she be so lucky? She had no idea but feared delving too deeply in case he changed his mind or she woke up from this beautiful dream to find herself still in New York, enslaved to a man whose touch made her skin crawl, her heart heavy and her mind numb.

Kenan sprang into his saddle then squinted at the sun.

"We'd best be getting back. It will be twilight soon and Rosie will be getting worried."

"Of course," Catherine agreed. Rosie was like a mother hen with her brothers. They were as important to the woman's existence as sun and water were to crops.

Kenan dug his feet into his mare's flanks and Catherine's own horse fell into the same steady rhythm as it trotted along behind.

They soon arrived at the farm and Catherine was surprised at how emotional she felt. It was like coming home to the only place she had ever really felt safe and secure. But she should not forget that this was not her home. This was the Duggan homestead and she was not a Duggan. She once would have been but that time had gone and though Kenan had told her that he loved her, he had not mentioned marriage or their future.

Her heartbeat quickened. In her joy at his passion, she had not considered the reality of the situation but now here it was, staring her harshly in the face like the midday sun. She was a harlot, she had been used by another man, and once folks heard about her return, there would be questions. How could she tell them the truth? And what was the alternative? If they believed her uncle's story that she'd been taken by the Indians then it would be even worse. She would forever be seen as tainted, like a spring where a dead animal's rotting flesh has poisoned the water.

It was rare that a woman taken by the tribal warriors ever returned. If they did, then most made their living as painted cats and never expected a good, decent man like Kenan to take them to wife. Locals would be shocked if Kenan did so and Catherine wondered if it was even fair to place him in that position. It would be wrong of her to expect him to take that upon himself and his family. It would not do. She would have to spare this good, honest and decent man from any slander and make the decision for him.

"Hey!" Kenan made her jump . "Are you okay?"

She forced a smile. "Yes. Of course."

She allowed him to help her dismount.

"I'll stable the horses then come wash up before dinner." He planted a kiss on her cheek. His lips were warm, his scent so familiar, that she felt the heaviness in her heart increase. She had been foolish to believe that she could really be his wife and take up her former place in his affections. He deserved better.

Catherine watched the man she loved disappear into the shadows of the barn then she trudged toward the little house, wondering how on earth she was going to summon the courage she needed to leave him again.

As soon as she opened the door, Rosie flew at her and hugged her close.

"Catherine! Did you have fun? Where's Kenan? What took you so long?"

The young woman pulled Catherine into the center of the room then took her face in her hands. She was as wholesome and kind-hearted as anyone could be. It was yet another reason why Catherine could not bring shame upon this family.

"Kenan is in the barn. What is it, Rosie? You look..." She searched for the right words as she stared into Rosie's warm amber eyes. They were illuminated as if someone had lit a fire in her belly and it glowed now, its flames flickering in her gaze.

"We've been invited to a wedding tomorrow!" Rosie giggled, now more like a sixteen year old than a woman just past thirty.

Catherine gasped as Rosie grabbed her hands and spun her around in a circle, jumping up and down as she did so.

"Rosie! Stop!"

"Oh! I'm so sorry, Catherine! I'm just so...so..." A crimson hue filled Rosie's cheeks.

"You're excited?" Catherine queried.

"Well, yes," She bit her lip. "I guess I am. It'll be such a grand fandango!"

"Who's getting married? And where?" Catherine squeezed Rosie's hands to convey her approval, allowing her own concerns to drift to the back of her mind.

"Billy Hampton's marrying Rita-Mae Hudson!" Rosie jumped up and down again.

"How do you know?" Catherine felt her heart lift at Rosie's infectious happiness.

Rosie lowered her eyes, suddenly coy. Her blush deepened and Catherine realized that the real reason for her friend's joy lay in the attentions of a man.

"Rosie?"

"It was Joshua Hampton. He rode out here this morning, not long after you'd gone."

"Joshua Hampton?"

"Yeah." Rosie released Catherine's hands and made a show of tidying her hair and tightening the pins that held it back from her face. "He rides with Kenan on the cattle trail. I...uh...we met last summer when he stopped by."

"And you..." Catherine laughed as she pointed at Rosie. "You like him!"

Rosie's eyes gleamed as she grinned back at Catherine. "I do! I really do! But it's foolish. I'm past being a wife...too old to be a mother!"

"Nonsense!" Catherine clicked her tongue. "You have plenty of time! Now, while your brother sorts the horses, come tell me all about this Joshua Hampton!"

Rosie followed her toward the kitchen table where Catherine listened with pleasure as her dear friend told her all about the man who had captured her own heart.

Chapter Seven

The wagon rattled along the rough path and Catherine swayed on the wooden boards that served as a seat, bumping against Rosie's side. She could feel the excitement bubbling in Kenan's sister at the prospect of seeing Joshua Hampton again. He had clearly made quite an impression upon Rosie and Catherine could see that she harbored hopes of a proposal of her own in the not too distant future. The aura around Rosie was so positive and so full of energy that Catherine allowed herself to bask in it so that it cheered her own soul and lifted her own sagging spirits. Though she had all but made up her mind that she could not—and should not—expect that Kenan would now take her to wife, she would savor the short time they had left together. She could take that at least to sustain her through the long hard winter of a lifetime that lay ahead.

"What is it, Catherine?" Rosie laid a cool hand upon her arm.

"Oh, nothing, really," she mumbled, realizing that she had been wringing her handkerchief in her lap. "I was just…"

"It's okay, sweeting." Rosie patted her hand. "That's all behind you now. You're back where you belong."

Catherine started at Rosie's words. Did she know what had happened to her? Though Catherine had told her friend a version of events, she had spared her the gritty details, fearing that the gentle woman's sensibilities would be shocked at the painful truth. Rosie was a good woman and she did not need to know about the horrors that existed out there in the wider world. Though Rosie had grown up in this wild young country of theirs, she had led a relatively protected life as the sweet, innocent daughter of her father and the sheltered sister to three strong, feisty brothers. The details of Catherine's time in New York would do nothing other than hurt and wound her friend.

"You do look fine this evening, Rosie!" Catherine sought to change the subject.

"I agree." Kenan grinned at her. He rode his mare alongside the wagon and Catherine's breath caught in her throat at how handsome he looked. He had on his Sunday best and had shaved his cheeks clean so that his dark mustache and the small triangle of beard that graced his chin stood out, making his eyes seem deeper and darker than usual.

He sat confidently in the saddle and he rested one hand upon his knee while he held the reins loosely in the other. He was in every way a strong, handsome, self-assured cowboy. The power of her emotions swept through her like a river that had burst its dam after heavy rainfall and her stomach flipped at the knowledge that she would soon be parted from him once more surged through her. Where would she find the strength to do it?

"Don't you think the honey satin suits my sister, Catherine?" Kenan smiled at Rosie, who bridled a little at his teasing.

"It really does," she replied and Rosie straightened in her seat, smoothing the full skirts of her gown out over her knees. "The color brings out the amber of her eyes."

The beautiful dress had actually belonged to Rosie's mother, packed away for years in a chest of precious things that the Duggan children had treasured. Kenan had been the one to suggest that his sister make use of their mother's clothing when she'd been in a panic about what to wear. It had not been easy for Rosie to don the gown, clearly she had wanted to protect her deceased mother's memories, but her brothers had insisted that they would like to see their mother's best clothes put to good use again. And who better to wear them than their darling Rosie?

So between them, Rosie and Catherine had adjusted the gown to fit Rosie's slender frame and she now looked every bit the lady.

"Are you sure?" Rosie asked Catherine for the hundredth time. "It's not too much? You know, I'm not used to such finery."

"You look beautiful." Catherine lifted Rosie's hand and planted a kiss upon her fingers. "Now stop fretting." She held her friend's hand tightly between her own, wondering at the strength beneath the red, work-worn skin.

As for Catherine, Rosie had gifted her a gown that she'd kept for best even though it had long been too short for the lithe young woman. It was made of the palest green cotton calico with a rounded neckline trimmed with a cream lace collar. She had giggled that afternoon with Rosie as they had to let out the bodice to accommodate Catherine's full bosom which had strained against the cool material. The real issue with the dress though had been the short bell sleeves which had left Catherine's scarred arms on display. Rosie had kindly removed a set of ruched lace sleeves from another dress then stitched them into the green calico.

Catherine had left her long, red hair down — the way Kenan liked it — in the fashion of a young, unmarried girl. Though she was far from virginal, she believed that her heart was pure and she wanted to allow herself the luxury of creating the outward illusion too.

Kenan winked at her then moved forwards to ride alongside Matthew. She smiled and relaxed against Rosie, watching her friend shake the reins to encourage Emmett's horse to move faster. The youngest Duggan had remained at the homestead for the evening, having picked the short straw. The animals needed watching as that afternoon, when Kenan had been checking the perimeter fencing, he'd found one of their chickens all torn up and half-eaten. It meant that there was likely a coyote in the vicinity and it would be back for a second helping.

Catherine gazed at the sun as it sank on the horizon behind the black tipped mountains. It looked as though the mountains themselves were on fire and the flames had scorched the peaks, leaving them the color of charcoal. The endless sky itself glowed crimson, amber and dusky pink. Its beauty was breathtaking. Looking at such splendor whilst resting her head upon the shoulder of a dear friend, Catherine wondered at how cruel life could be. With so much to appreciate in this fleeting human life, it was difficult to comprehend how there could be such pain and suffering.

If she were as innocent as she had been just two years ago, as innocent as Rosie seemed to be, then she would have enjoyed the stunning view without hindrance. But now, physically and emotionally scarred by life and mankind, the beauty was all the more poignant. She could see it, appreciate it and savor it. But a part of her heart lay heavy, for she knew that she would never be totally free to relish the splendor that life and nature had to offer. Her vision of the world had changed.

* * * *

Kenan reined in his mare as the magnificent Lone Wolf Ranch came into sight. Its buildings and fences stretched out for miles across the Montana grasslands, where the pale butter-colored sweet clover danced in the wind that swept the open plains.

The owner of the ranch, Dylan Hampton, had arrived in America with empty pockets and an even emptier belly just twenty years earlier, but he'd been stalwart and determined and he'd built himself a grand business that he had every right to be proud of.

He owned over ten thousand cattle, including a herd of Texas Longhorns, and he traded his beasts all over the western states. He had a bubbly, buxom wife who'd provided him with ten strong children, ranging from thirty five to just sixteen. Kenan supposed that access to good meat probably helped with the child rearing, as well as all that fresh Montana air. Children born into poverty were often so much weaker, especially those in the cow towns who were exposed to all manners of diseases brought in with the never ending deluge of immigrants. With so many new settlers arriving from as far as China, it was going to take a while for folks to build up immunity to the variety of infectious complaints that so often ailed them.

"So are we all set for a wedding?" Kenan smiled at Catherine.

She returned his smile but it didn't meet her eyes and he felt his spirits sag. He knew that this evening would not be easy for her but he also knew that hiding away would not help either. It would be like branding cattle, better to get it over and done with quickly than to dally around, allowing the poor cows' fears to build to a blind terror. Short and sharp was best. Let people see her, know that she was back and that she was here to stay. His own guts churned at the prospect of taking her into company but it was a happy occasion and he hoped that folks would be accepting, if not overly courteous.

He pulled his horse alongside the wagon and looked at Catherine. She leaned against Rosie, her eyes veiled as if deep in contemplation. Her shawl hung loosely around her arms and she looked like a fiery angel with her flame colored tresses tumbling down over her shoulders. Kenan was certain that she could have been plucked straight out of the sunset, so resplendent was her hair. Her dress was the color of fresh spring grass and it brought out the bright green of her eyes. Surely anyone could see that she was an innocent young woman, as pure as the first snowflakes of winter, though he feared that she might be as fragile, apt to melt away when she fell against the rocky ground. She'd been so strong, so brave, but trauma could cause cracks in a person that wouldn't always show immediately, and Kenan hoped that Catherine wasn't secretly crumbling inside.

They rode along the sandy path that took them up to the impressive homestead, then Kenan and Matthew tethered the horses to rest and graze.

"Pretty fine, huh?" Matthew mumbled then let out a whistle of awe.

"It is indeed, brother." Kenan patted his shoulder. "We'll have all this one day. Just you wait and see!"

Matthew threw his head back and laughed. "Sure we will, Kenan! Sure we will!"

Kenan suppressed the urge to say more. He had been saving hard and knew that if he got another year of cattle driving under his belt, he too would be able to invest in some cattle of his own and to develop their own homestead. He was keeping it quiet for now though, not wanting to raise anyone's hopes until he felt sure that he could make the dream a reality. Too many folks had hopes and dreams of owning their own land then building their own empires but all too often they were just dreams. The bottle, women or the gambling tables came calling and their hard earned savings were squandered away like dust blown away on the plains. But not Kenan. He had no time for such frivolities and he'd stashed away every penny he could spare.

"Ladies." Kenan held out his arm for Catherine and helped her down from the wagon.

She tucked her small hand into the crook of his elbow and he covered it with his own, squeezing her fingers to reassure her. Rosie took Matthew's arm, then the four of them climbed the wide whitewashed steps that led to the expansive front porch, talking and laughing as free and dandy as if nothing had – or ever would – give them a moment's strife.

The door was opened by a smartly dressed young man, whom Catherine took to be one of the Hampton brothers, and they were invited into a spacious reception room. It was certainly an impressive place and she had to grit her teeth to keep her mouth closed. The wooden lounge area was warm and clean with solid pine furniture, upholstered with a damask satin material. There were four large chairs, two at either side of the enormous fireplace where a fire now blazed, even though it was not yet dark and it was clear that this room was not used for cooking. The seats were equipped with plump matching damask pillows, which Catherine guessed were filled with duck down or horsehair. A chaise longue ran alongside the wide window that opened onto the land behind the house, and several small side tables were dotted about. It reminded her of the parlors of the New York upper class, though it was larger and airier and certainly not as claustrophobic. The stuffy rooms of the city had been full of scornful folks and their derisive snorts, which usually occurred when they found out that she was from the outskirts of Virginia City.

"Thanks for coming," the handsome young man spoke, his attention focused on Rosie.

Catherine looked from the man to Rosie then back again. Rosie's cheeks flushed crimson as if she'd stood too long in the sun and Catherine realized that this must have been the subject of her affections.

"Catherine," Kenan broke the awkward silence. "This is Joshua Hampton. We've been on the same team on several cattle drives."

Catherine smiled at Joshua as he took her hand and bowed over it.

"As you can see" — Kenan frowned in mock disapproval — "he's quite the charmer."

"Pleased to meet you." Catherine inclined her head, keen to show good manners to the man who'd stolen Rosie's heart.

"So you're Catherine Montgomery?" Joshua's curious eyes made her stomach flip. What had he heard about her?

"Yes," Kenan broke in. "This is Miss Montgomery."

"Well I'm mighty glad to make your acquaintance!"

Catherine stared at him, wondering if he was mocking her. She glanced at Rosie but her friend was smiling adoringly at Joshua. He must be genuine.

Kenan gently placed a hand in the small of her back. The heat of his touch seared through her dress and it seemed that his warmth spread out over her skin, healing and reassuring as it traveled. She wanted to feel his presence at her side always, to know that he was with her, supporting her and loving her every day until the sun set on the horizon. Kenan held the key to her happiness and she knew that if she lost him, it would remain forever locked.

"Catherine?" Kenan called her name. He pointed toward the others, who were moving through the room and toward an open door way off to the right. "They're making their way outside. Are you okay?"

Tears stung her eyes and she had to blink hurriedly to clear them away.

"What is it? Are you sick?" He squeezed her elbow. When she looked up, his face was creased with concern.

"No." She shook her head. "No, I'm okay. I was just thinking about you... I mean about us...I mean...how it could have been."

"Hush, now." He leaned forward and planted a soft kiss upon her lips. It was the gentlest brush of his skin against hers, yet her body responded instantly and she swayed toward him, planting her hands flat against his broad chest. The familiar fire began to burn in her belly and a shiver of desire ran up her spine.

"Let's enjoy the evening, Catherine, and help the happy couple celebrate. There's plenty of time to think on the past. Please try to enjoy the here and now."

She inhaled deeply of his delicious masculine scent. It was as fresh and clear as the morning forests after heavy rainfall, when the sweet pine and fresh sage rose into the air and mingled with the aroma of the damp earth and the heady pollen of thousands of flowers. It lifted her spirits. Her heart beat faster and for a moment she felt as if she would faint. Not being able to inhale his scent, to touch his skin or to feel his heart beat beneath her hand would be too much to bear and she cursed destiny for stealing away the life she had longed for. It wasn't fair! She had sacrificed her marriage and her plans and she had hurt the man she'd loved with all of her heart in the process. Having been parted from him once had been agony — a second time would be excruciating torment.

"Come on, you two!" Rosie called from the doorway, her eyes illuminated with love and excitement, optimism and hope. Though Catherine wished that she, too, had the same look in her eyes, she would not be jealous of Rosie's joy. She breathed deeply and steeled herself to face the evening, whatever it might bring.

* * * *

The wedding ceremony passed in a flurry of solemn words and giggled promises. Kenan had sat close to Catherine on one of the benches laid out at the rear of the homestead. The low wooden seats had been placed in rows to create an aisle like that of a church. The Hamptons had gone all out for this celebration of their son's joining in matrimony to the young woman he'd chosen to take to wife. She came from Virginia City. She was the daughter of the schoolmaster. Her father was well connected, though he lived modestly, and Rita-Mae Hudson was sure to inherit a substantial fortune one day. It made her a good choice for twenty-two year old Billy Hampton, though he looked as keen as mustard to be marrying the buxom wench.

Kenan estimated her to be about eighteen at most and by the looks of her, she was either a little plump or several months along with child. That would explain the shotgun wedding. It hadn't been mentioned the last time he'd seen Joshua but evidently, Rita-Mae's expanding waistline had brought it forwards.

He felt Catherine's knee bump against his own and he nudged back. She slipped him a sideways smile. The evening air was warm and fragrant with the scent of the wild flowers that had been tied to the ends of the benches. The sun had almost set and the flattened lawn area was gently lit with kerosene lamps which hung from strategically placed posts. The bride and groom had walked along it together just twenty minutes ago and the guests had sighed with approval at the handsome young couple. When they'd passed, Kenan had stolen a glance at Catherine and been saddened to see a shadow passing over her face. She'd masked it pretty rapidly but it had hurt him to see it. Clearly, she was still in pain and grieved for what had been lost. Darn it, it made him furious to think about how it could have been and how that had all been taken away by a drunken old fool and a greedy son of a bitch shipping tycoon, but he wasn't sure how to put it all right...or if it ever could be. All he knew for sure was that he loved Catherine and wanted to spend as much time with her as he could. He'd try not to think on what came after that. His soul was still too bruised by his desire for vengeance and the righting of wrongs to be healing—at least not yet.

He also wasn't sure if he was thinking straight. His physical attraction to Catherine was so powerful that it reminded him of a steam train thundering along a track. It smoked and chugged, drowning out everything else with its noise and well stoked fire, oblivious to all sense and reason, impervious to the hoots of coyotes and the arrows of Indian warriors. Just being near her right now heated his blood and forced all rational thought from his brain. All he could think about was being with her, lying with her and taking her completely. In fact, he didn't think he'd be able to wait until they made it home.

* * * *

Catherine sipped the mulled cider slowly, forcing herself not to gulp it down. It was warm and spicy with cinnamon and she wanted to keep tasting it, filling her mouth with it until its potency numbed her senses and warmed her throughout.

Kenan had excused himself and Matthew was circulating amongst the other guests. It was a big wedding with about seventy guests in all but then the families had money and were keen to celebrate that fact.

"So, what do you think?" Rosie clinked her tankard against Catherine's. "Isn't it just the finest wedding you've ever attended?"

"I've not been to many." Catherine frowned. "Most folks don't have the means to make such a fandango about it."

"That's true," Rosie agreed. "Last wedding I went to was in the small wooden church in Virginia City and there were ten at most there. The preacher was passing through and he had to complete six ceremonies before he moved on again. Most of the brides were, of course, expecting..."

Catherine smiled. At least a third of all young women getting hitched were carrying their first child. That was why when a preacher stopped in a town, he was often busy for twelve hours straight. Virginia City, however, had now secured her own man of the cloth and Reverend Felshaw was happy to oblige those preferring to marry at their homesteads—providing they made a generous donation to his upkeep, of course.

Right now, the Reverend was filling his ruddy cheeks with the roasted hog that had been cooked on a turning spit over an open fire. He chewed and drank in turns, throwing back mulled cider like it was the elixir of everlasting life.

"Will it be you next then, Rosie?"

Rosie turned wide eyes to Catherine.

"Pardon?"

"Will you be the next Hampton bride?"

"I..." Rosie's mouth hung open and Catherine felt instantly ashamed. She knew that her friend would have told her about any proposal. "I don't know. I mean, it hasn't been discussed."

"Of course." Catherine squeezed Rosie's arm. "I didn't mean anything by it. I just hope that it will be. I long to see you happy."

Rosie looked at Catherine for a long moment then took her face in her hands.

"That is what I want for you too, my friend, and for Kenan, of course."

Catherine gazed into the amber eyes that were as warm and sincere as Kenan's, yet softer and lighter. If only Rosie could have her wish but that would be more than Catherine dared hope for.

Chapter Eight

As the drinks flowed, the wedding party got into full swing. The benches were cleared away and the posts with the kerosene lamps were moved to create a wide circle. A few of the male guests went into the house then reappeared with musical instruments which they set about tuning before launching into a lively Irish jig. The bride and groom took to the floor and the guests and families laughed and clapped as the handsome young couple whirled around and around in time to the music. Before long, they were joined by other couples and soon the whole circle was filled with drunken, boisterous movement and laughter.

Catherine moved away from the circle and into the shadows where she stood and gazed at the joy before her. It was so good to see such innocent happiness, such carefree enjoyment. It lifted her own spirits and made her feel buoyant, like driftwood bobbing along on the river in the warm sunshine, though she knew that at any moment a cloud could cover the sun or she could hit a whirlpool and be dragged into the swirling depths and buried forever. It was knowing this that made her pleasure all the sweeter—because it was fleeting, temporary and fragile.

"Will you dance?" Kenan's breath was hot against her cheek, his hands firm as he squeezed her shoulders.

"I can think of something that I'd prefer to be doing." She laughed, the cider making her bold and amorous.

"Well in that case"–he took her hand then pulled her after him—"you'd better follow me."

She hurried along behind him, leaving the hoots and hollers of the wedding party safely ensconced within the circle of lights. As they moved away, it grew darker and cooler and she welcomed the refreshing night air as it soothed her hot cheeks and gently dried the fine sheen of perspiration that had gathered above her top lip. She hadn't realized how warm it had been around all of those people but now it was obvious and she was glad to be away from them.

Kenan stopped when they rounded a corner and were out of the sight of the wedding party. When he had checked that they were alone, he took hold of her and pushed her backwards against the side of the house. The sun had warmed the wood throughout the summer day and the logs now gave up some of that heat to Catherine, their warmth penetrating the thin material of her gown. It made her think of how Kenan warmed her with his presence and his attentions and how she absorbed his offerings, unable to generate her own heat like a tree cut down in its prime.

"You are so beautiful." Kenan took her chin gently between his thumb and forefinger.

The full moon sat directly above them and Catherine imagined that it was looking down on them, wondering what their next move would be. She gasped as Kenan started to unbutton her dress. He slid each button slowly, yet deftly, from its hole and she held her breath in anticipation.

When her dress lay open to the waist, he slid his hands in and parted it so that her corset and chemise were exposed.

"Such big bouncy tits." He licked his lips before lowering his head to her chest where he rubbed his face over the heavy mounds of her flesh. Her belly flipped with excitement and she grabbed the back of his head, pressing his face into her and moaning when he covered her erect nipples with his mouth and suckled them in turn through the gauzy material. He pulled first on one, taking it deep into his mouth and running his hot tongue over the tip, before turning his attention to the other one, until Catherine felt the flutter deep in her core that reminded her of that link between breast and womb.

He continued toying with her in this way and she felt her desire for him building inside her until she was so full of need that she believed she would explode. When he stopped for a moment to look into her eyes, she quickly slipped her damp chemise down over her breasts so that the rosy buds stood to attention in the moonlight and basked under the heat of Kenan's gaze.

He leaned forward and kissed her whilst he moved his hands over her naked flesh, pinching and rolling her hard nubs between his fingertips until she didn't know whether it was pleasure or pain that stirred the juices in her cunny.

"I need to take you," Kenan mumbled between kisses.

Catherine massaged his tongue with her own then lowered her hands to his groin and caressed his bulging cock. It was hard and swollen beneath the material of his trousers and she could feel its energy, waiting to be released.

Kenan grabbed her by the shoulders and spun her round so that she faced the side of the house. "Like this," he ordered, pushing her upper body toward the wooden wall so that her exposed bosoms grazed the logs. He kept one hand on her back so that she stayed in place while he popped open his trousers and freed his erection from his underwear. Catherine reached around to take him in her hand and she moaned at the size and girth of his excitement.

She held onto him and squeezed, sliding her hand backwards until she held him at the base and could cup his balls with her fingers. Her touch spurred him onwards and he lifted her skirts up around her waist then whipped her bloomers down. There was a moment's pause then she felt a sharp twinge as Kenan gave her bottom a quick slap.

"Ouch!" she grunted in surprise rather than pain.

"Sorry," he chuckled, "I couldn't resist. Your behind looks so pert and delicious in the moonlight that I just had to."

"It's okay." She was aroused by his approval and curious at her own reaction.

Then her breasts met the wood full on as he shoved her forwards by the shoulders and she felt his rigid member pulsing next to the flesh of her bottom. The logs rubbed her naked chest, their bumps and grooves caressing her tender nipples like a rough and inexperienced lover. Kenan held her waist with one hand while he ran his manhood over the tops of her thighs then slipped it between them. As he pushed, she gasped, thinking that he would enter her behind.

"Kenan!" Her voice cracked with uncertainty as he moved over her tight flesh, pressing the opening that had never been entered.

"It's okay, my love. I'm just so eager to take you." He laughed softly then used a foot to push her legs further apart. When his erection met her welcoming silken folds, she shivered then tipped her hips toward him to allow him to enter. He gave a quick thrust and plunged into her in one go.

As he moved deeply within her, she met his rhythm and they became one, gathering speed until they met the beat of the *bodhrán* being played around the corner. The musicians upped the tempo and Kenan met their pace, his flesh filling Catherine, then withdrawing, then filling her again. Each time he entered her fully, the tip of his member met her cervix and the sensation was at once painful yet erotic. It seemed to send echoes rebounding deep inside her that rang out like the hoots of the excited dancers.

Over the music, she could hear their combined breathing, deep, lusty and primitive. They became united in their need and Catherine groaned as her body climbed the mountain of desire. The pine chafing her nipples, the fingers that she slid down to her sex and rubbed over the swelling bud that lay just above Kenan's thrusting cock, and the stretching and plundering of her sex all combined to send her screaming and throbbing over the abyss. She bucked up and down in wild abandon as her lover grew inside her suddenly then pulsed into her, filling her with his hot seed.

When their bodies had slowed and their breathing grew shallower, Kenan slipped out of her then rested his head upon her shoulder. She leaned her head to the side so that it touched his. Her heart swelled with love and joy, full of the ecstasy of their lovemaking and she knew with all certainty, that whatever the bride and groom got up to that night, it would pale in comparison with the passion that she and Kenan had just shared.

* * * *

"You go first." Kenan nudged her in front of him as they approached the wedding party. The bride and groom had now been hoisted onto the shoulders of their family members and they were being paraded around like a prize heifer and bull.

Catherine smoothed out her skirts then flashed Kenan a quick smile before she walked into the circle of light. Her cheeks were hot and flushed and she felt as if everyone must have known where she had been and what she had been doing. Yet as she cast a discreet glance around her, she noted that all eyes were upon the newlyweds.

"Catherine!" Rosie's eyes shined with cider and excitement. Her ebony hair had been pinned neatly at the nape of her neck earlier that evening but it now hung loose, its waves tumbling seductively down over her shoulders, gleaming like the wings of a raven. Catherine could see why Rosie had captured the attention of Joshua Hampton. Though he currently had one of his brother's muscular buttocks perched upon his shoulder, and was cheering and laughing at the bawdy comments of the inebriated men, Catherine saw that Joshua regularly checked that Rosie was still watching him and his face lit up when he found that she was.

"You really like him, huh?" Catherine leaned closer to Rosie to be heard over the tinny chords of the banjo.

Rosie grinned. "I can't help myself, Catherine! He's just..." She twirled glossy strands of hair between her fingers.

"It's okay!" Catherine laughed. "I understand!"

She tucked her arm into Rosie's and tapped her foot in time to the music. It felt so good to be happy. She had just made love with the man she adored, she was celebrating a wedding with her best friend whilst watching that friend fall deeply in love and, for once in a very long time, she felt her spirit lifting. It was so darned good to be alive!

"Come on!" Catherine pulled Rosie away from the edge of the circle and right into its center. Then she hitched up her skirts above her ankles and began to kick up her legs.

"Catherine!" Rosie giggled.

"Dance!" Catherine ordered, almost doubled up with laughter as Rosie tried to copy her movements.

Catherine's heart beat merrily, her eyes glinted with joy and she twirled around with her friend, lost for a wonderful moment in the sheer pleasure of being human.

Kenan took a big gulp of sweet cider to quench the thirst he'd just worked up with Catherine. His lust for her seemed to be increasing. He couldn't understand it but he didn't want to over analyze it either. He felt so good, so carefree right now. It could be the amazing sex, the strong cider and the balmy evening air but he knew that it was more complicated than that. It was due to Catherine's delightful presence—her return to his life, to be by his side...where she belonged.

As he watched her now, careering around with Rosie to the lively music, his heart swelled with joy. He could almost pretend that none of it had ever happened. Maybe, he reasoned, he actually could do that. What was stopping him? If Catherine could move on, could forget, then maybe he could too. As she skipped and looped in a figure of eight, her cheeks glowed and her hair flowed down her back like a ruby waterfall. It caught the light from the kerosene lamps and seemed like sultry flames bursting forth from the head of the most beautiful angel he could imagine. He laughed softly, wondering if the cider was affecting his vision. But no, she truly was breathtakingly gorgeous. She had such an innocent, pure face yet such a curvaceous, decadent body. He felt the heat of lust begin to rise between his legs and he looked away, trying to think about something else, anything else, before he had an uncomfortable bulge in his trousers.

As he gazed across the circle of people and off into the darkness beyond the immediate garden area, something caught his eye. It was something he hadn't expected to see tonight—hell, not any night. And it was something that bothered him greatly. He slammed his tankard down on the table next to him then marched off into the darkness, grim determination taking a steely hold on his features.

A figure appeared to be flying across the fields toward him. Illuminated by moonlight, it looked like a wild specter, a grisly spirit sent to haunt the land of the living. Kenan's heart beat increased and though he felt like turning and running away, he kept walking toward it, the distance between them disappearing like sand into a hole.

The closer he got to the figure, the more frightening it appeared. Wild white hair was given a silvery glow by the full moon. Its face was gray as parchment, its eyes feral black hollows. The comforting sound of the music got further away as the terrifying creature got nearer and Kenan reached down to feel the reassuring presence of his gun.

But then he stopped, reality overwhelming him. He shook his head to clear it of his irrational, superstitious thoughts then looked again.

It was an old woman hurrying toward him, waving her arms and shouting for help. He started walking again then broke into a jog.

He stopped just in front of her.

"What in hell are you doing out here on your own?" He grabbed the woman's shoulders as if to shake her but then changed his mind. Catherine's aunt was sobbing as if her heart would break and she struggled to catch her breath.

"Hey, now, Mrs Montgomery," he soothed as he looked into the woman's tear-filled eyes. "Calm yourself down."

The woman's mouth opened and closed like a landed fish, struggling to hold onto life.

"I...I've been... He's...he's gone!"

"What are you talking about, woman?" Kenan frowned.

"My husband! He's gone!"

Kenan swallowed an unsavory comment, aware that it wouldn't help the situation but his mind bubbled with possibilities. Had the old goat done a runner? Had he heard that Catherine had returned and now he couldn't bear to face her or did he fear Kenan's reaction? Surely the old man must have realized that

Kenan would come for him once he knew that he'd sold Catherine to save his own skin?

"Please, Mr Duggan!" The woman pounded her gnarled old hands upon his chest and Kenan looked down at them with repulsion. He hadn't remembered Edie Montgomery being so aged. Had the past two years really taken such a toll on her?

"Okay, okay." He took hold of her hands then lowered them. "Where has Mr Montgomery gone?"

"We were on our way here... He was feeling better this morning and he wanted to come. He seemed...well...normal, like his old self."

"I don't understand." Kenan scowled at her. "What do you mean...normal?"

As if William Montgomery could ever be described as normal. What kind of man sold his niece then lied to her fiancé about it? Catherine's uncle had destroyed her life as well as Kenan's. To do what he had done, to be so cold and self-serving, so oblivious to the emotions of those around him, took a cold heart indeed. So no, he could not accept that William had ever been normal.

"He's not been the man I married, this past year. It's like it all welled up inside him...all that he did..." She bit her lip, suddenly aware that she had nearly said something that could get her husband into trouble.

"I know what he did." Kenan snapped.

"Oh my!" she gasped. "Mr Duggan! Kenan! I am so sorry! I—"

"Save it for later!" he spat. "Now what's the problem with your husband?"

"We were on our way to the ceremony. I was so happy that he seemed back to his old self. You can't imagine what it's been like, Mr Duggan, losing him for days at a time—"

"How dare you!" Kenan's hands became fists as fury rose in his belly. "How dare you tell me that I don't know what it's like to lose someone!"

"Oh...I'm so sorry...I just meant that with William it's so strange." She wrung her hands. "One day he's rational, practical and sensible then the next he's like a stranger. He either thinks that we're courting and still in our first flush of youth or he imagines that I'm his mother." Her lower lip trembled. "And sometimes...he doesn't recognize me at all!" She burst into fresh tears.

Kenan glared at the woman but in spite of his anger, he pitied her. He wasn't quite sure what she meant about William Montgomery but it didn't sound nice. He'd suffered the pain of loss and grief, thinking Catherine was dead for so long. But this was clearly different. Edie Montgomery had her husband's physical presence but not his mental one.

She blew her nose loudly on a handkerchief she'd pulled from her bell sleeve then wiped her eyes. A strange calm seemed to fall over her and she raised her red and swollen eyes to Kenan's face.

"Mr Duggan." She tilted her head to one side. "You said that you know about what happened."

"I do." He ground his teeth together.

"But how?"

He noted that the fear he'd seen in her eyes just moments ago had been replaced by a calculating coldness and he wondered again at how far this woman had been involved in the events surrounding Catherine's disappearance. His stomach churned and ice crept into his veins. Had she really loved Catherine as she'd claimed or had she been jealous of the young redhead and wanted her out of the way? Edie's own beauty had faded, so maybe she didn't like

Catherine's presence as a constant reminder of how her own youth had long since deserted her.

He decided to keep Catherine's return a secret for now.

"A preacher who'd passed through New York had bumped into her," he lied, watching for her reaction. "I told him all about my flame haired fiancée, *kidnapped...*" He emphasized the last word then paused. "Kidnapped by the Indians. He informed me about such a beauty who'd appeared suddenly in the city and told him one night of her plight."

"Oh." The woman roamed his face with wild eyes. "I see."

"So" —he pulled his Stetson lower over his eyes— "you were telling me about William."

"Yes!" She fluttered her hand over her chest. "William!" She seemed to suddenly remember her husband. "He's gone! He stopped the wagon about a mile down the road. He started..." Her cheeks filled with color which appeared black in the shadows of the night.

"He started what, Ma'am?"

"Kissing me."

"How's that unusual? Ain't a man allowed to kiss his wife now?"

"Well, he...he doesn't do that sort of thing anymore. Hasn't for some time. Not since his mind started to wander." She frowned then laid a hand on Kenan's chest. "I was shocked and I jumped. He got mad and he..." She burst into fresh tears. "He jumped from the wagon and ran off!"

"I see. And do you have any idea where he's gone?"

"I watched him for a while and called out to him but he soon disappeared. I'm worried, Mr Duggan!

There's wild animals out there and he didn't have his pistol. I hid it when he started getting sick."

"So whadda you want me to do about his disappearance?" Kenan demanded. "After what happened to Catherine, why in the hell do you think I would help you out?"

She moved her hand against his chest and he fought the urge to slap it away.

"I understand your anger, Mr Duggan, I really do. But he's all I have left. Please." She fluttered her eyelashes. "Please help me to find him."

Kenan sighed then took hold of her hand and put it from him.

"Okay, I'll help. But I ain't making no promises. It's pitch black out there and he could have gone in any direction. Hell! I hope that he ain't gone off into the cattle pen."

He stared into the darkness as if trying to work out which direction William had taken but though the moon was full, the wind had picked up and it carried thick clouds along with it, as if playing a game of hide and seek with the land. Kenan turned to the woman trembling at his side.

"Well, Mrs Montgomery, I think we'd best get you over to the crowd though I ask that you do nothing to ruin the joy of the bride and groom. I'll see if I can round up a few of the men then we'll go look for William."

"Thank you Mr Duggan."

He walked quickly, keen to maintain a pace that left her trailing in his wake. He didn't want her at his side when he saw Catherine. He had to warn her first. Edie Montgomery hadn't even known that Catherine had returned and he realized that Catherine had wanted it that way. She clearly needed some time to think before she met up with her aunt and uncle again and no wonder. After what they'd put her through, he wouldn't blame Catherine if she never wanted to see them ever again.

Blind fury surged, then roared in his veins. He couldn't deny that he now had the perfect opportunity to get revenge. William Montgomery was losing his mind according to his wife. He was gone in the head and he'd wandered off into the night. Anything could happen to him out there. Anything! And nobody would have to know about it. His blood flowed like fire through his body and his heart thrummed with the call for vengeance. They had taken Catherine away from him, leaving him broken with grief, whilst she'd been thrust into the arms of a man who sought to hurt her and had branded her like a cow with a white-hot knife.

Kenan realized that tonight had brought him an opportunity for retribution. It was not only William Montgomery who'd changed. Kenan had changed, too, and he was no longer the man he'd once been. In fact, he doubted that he even got the flashes of his old self in the same way as Catherine's uncle did. Kenan's innocence was gone and he didn't know if anything would ever bring it back.

Chapter Nine

Catherine finished twirling then let down her skirts. Laughing and breathing heavily, she leaned on Rosie's shoulder.

"That was fun!"

"Just like old times." Rosie giggled. "You sure can dance."

"Why thank you, kind lady." Catherine dropped into a mock curtsey, bowing her head low as she did so. When she raised her eyes, still smiling, to meet Rosie's gaze, her laughter died in her throat. "What is it, Rosie?"

Kenan's twin sister stared off into the distance, beyond the circle of celebration and into the darkness.

"Catherine," Rosie whispered. "Is that your aunt with Kenan?"

"I..." Catherine's mouth went dry. "I think it is."

"Why would she be here...at this time of night?"

Catherine shrugged. She felt like a goose had walked over her grave and an icy hand seemed to grip her spine. She hadn't seen her aunt since her return and if she was totally honest, she hadn't wanted to. Not being reunited with Edie and William had been a way of trying to move on, to put what had happened behind her. Though the events immediately prior to her time in New York, as well as the two years she'd spent there, were never far from her mind, not being near the people who had instigated her departure made it seem less real. Her brief time with Kenan had made her feel better, almost like the Catherine she had been, but she knew that as soon as she looked into her aunt's eyes, or heard her uncle's voice, she would likely crumble.

"Rosie, please help me," she choked out. "I can't see her."

Rosie turned to her. "Whadda you mean?"

"I just...I'm not ready..." She raised a trembling hand to her brow and smoothed the beads of perspiration away.

"Of course." Rosie looked around them. "Don't worry, Catherine. You don't have to see her right now. Lord in Heaven, whatever did they do to you?" She took hold of Catherine's arm then led her away from the celebrations and toward the house, only stopping to whisper into Matthew's ear. Catherine watched as a frown passed over his face then he walked toward Kenan.

"Matthew!" Kenan reached out to grip his brother's shoulder. He couldn't explain it but he was so glad to see him.

"Kenan." Matthew leaned close to him. "Can I have a word?"

"Sure. Excuse me."

Edie Montgomery scowled but walked a little way off, feigning interest in the fauna.

"Rosie just told me that she saw you and Mrs Montgomery approaching. Catherine got jittery so she's taken her into the house. Seems your lady friend wasn't too keen to speak to her aunt. Any particular reason why?"

"It's a long story, Matthew. I'll explain another time. Is Catherine okay though?" His stomach churned as he thought of her having to see the woman who'd allowed her to enter a living hell.

"She didn't look too good but Rosie'll take care of her."

"Sure." Catherine was in good hands. He'd deal with old William Montgomery then he'd seek out Catherine and hold her tight, make her feel safe as he longed to do.

"So why's she here?" Matthew gestured at Edie.

"She was on her way here with William earlier this evening when he took sick. She claims he's not been himself recently and that his mind wanders. Apparently"–Kenan felt a grin twitching at the corners of his mouth at the ridiculousness of the situation– "he tried to romance her on the journey."

Matthew shook his head and tutted.

"So she declined his attentions and he jumped out of the wagon then ran off. She says she was screaming his name for ages but he just ignored her. I don't know what to make of it."

"So you wanna go look for him?" Matthew lifted one dark eyebrow.

"Better had." Kenan knew that he had to ask for assistance to find old Montgomery, that it was nigh impossible to think he'd find him alone but really he just wanted to set out unhindered so that he could find the old man and –

"What is it?" Matthew's face was etched with concern.

"I'm just...worried is all, Matthew. Can you see if you can round up a few others? Less drunk ones of course." He attempted a smile but it felt like a bitter grin.

"Of course," Matthew replied.

"Be discreet!" Kenan muttered. "We don't wanna ruin the wedding party."

He stood and watched as Matthew made his way around the guests, selecting a few of the more sober men. Edie Montgomery appeared at his side.

"Will they help?" She sounded tired, almost defeated.

"I guess so," Kenan responded as his brother headed back toward him followed by four other men. Each one bore the signs of a night spent drinking and dancing—flushed cheeks, sweaty brow, disheveled clothing and wide relaxed smiles.

When they stood in front of him he gave them a hasty debrief then sent two of them to fetch kerosene lamps from the house.

"Mrs Montgomery." Kenan took her arm. "You'd better go over there and wait with the others. No sense in you trailing around in the darkness and getting injured now is there?"

Her eyes flashed with irritation but she inclined her head. "If that is what you think to be best, Mr Duggan. But please...please find my husband and bring him back safely to me."

"I'll do my best, ma'am." Kenan tweaked the brim of his hat.

He would do his best, but not to bring the old man safely back. Anything could happen out there in the darkness. A pistol could go off accidentally. A wild animal could spring from nowhere, disturbed by drunken men staggering around, and that beast could attack the nearest—and most vulnerable—man.

Hell, who knew? Anything could happen.

The men returned with lamps and their weapons and Kenan took one of the former then unholstered his own gun.

"Come on then, fellas! We're looking for William Montgomery. According to his ol' lady he's none too sharp at the moment. Take care not to shoot him for a coyote!"

Matthew walked at his side and the men followed. He led them away from the celebrations, away from humanity and toward his own private mission for revenge.

When they reached the dark, bulky shapes of the outbuildings, Kenan handed Matthew the lamp before he divided the men into three separate search parties. He waved the first off to the left, the second straight ahead, then he led Matthew off to the right in the direction of the fields where Edie Montgomery had pointed.

He stood still for a moment, watching the small circles of light cast by the lamps as they drifted away. The moon sat almost directly above him, shining like a new silver penny, pure, untainted and innocent. He'd looked up at that same moon thousands of times during his lifetime and many times with joy in his heart but now he realized that there had probably been many more times with a heart full of sorrow.

"What is it Kenan?" Matthew asked. "Are we really going after William Montgomery just to rescue him?"

Kenan looked down at the grass at his feet. It was bathed in the cold moonlight and he shivered, wondering for a moment how spilled blood would seem in that ethereal glow. It would probably appear black, and that seemed appropriate because right now his heart felt black as a thundercloud.

"Please don't ask me anymore, Matthew. I don't wanna lie to you." Kenan held his brother's curious gaze. "I have something I have to do. I don't even know yet..." He looked down at his hands. "I don't even know if I can do it. All I do know is that I have to do something. I have to put this sorry mess right or I'll never be able to move on."

"Are you sure that this is the right thing, Kenan?"

Matthew's eyes were wide and sincere and held no judgment. Kenan knew that his brother trusted him totally and that whatever it was that he decided to do, Matthew would be by his side, true and firm.

"I'm not sure that I know what the right thing is anymore, Matthew." He holstered his gun, removed his hat then ran a hand through his damp hair. "I wish I did but..."

"Come on then." Matthew squeezed his shoulder. "Let's start looking then we can take it as it comes. Whatever it is, you'll work it out."

Kenan smiled gratefully at Matthew's practical approach then put his Stetson back on.

"Oh Mr Montgomery!" he called out into the darkness, cupping his hands around his mouth to send his voice further. "Mr Montgomery! Are you out there? It's Kenan Duggan! We're here to help you get...safely home."

Kenan held up a hand to stop Matthew in his tracks. They were making their way toward a large outdoor pen where the cattle had been secured for the night. The heat from the animal bodies drifted toward him through the wooden fencing and the aroma from their cooling flesh was at once sharp yet comforting. It was the smell he worked with daily, the warm mixture of grass and mud, honey and tin.

As the clouds danced across the moon, the cows seemed to be participating in an elaborate show, each one revealed then hidden in turn. Though there were several hundred head of cattle in the pen, they still had enough space to walk around and graze when they chose, but right now they were still and calm. Some of them stood but some lay on the grassy ground, awkwardly posed as if their legs had been chopped from beneath them. It made Kenan think of a graveyard where folks were placed for their eternal rest. He shivered at the maudlin direction of his ponderings.

Looking at their lassitude made Kenan feel suddenly weary and he wished that he could hurry home to bed where he would hold Catherine against his chest, his face buried in the crimson waves of her hair. He would sleep like that all night, entwined with his lover until the sun rose. It took all of his strength to stay rooted to the spot, to fight the urge to run back to the house and seek out the woman he loved. But if he did that, he knew that matters would still remain unresolved and he would still be unable to settle.

"What was that?" Matthew whispered urgently, pointing in the direction of the gate to the pen.

Kenan shook his head. He couldn't see past the huge bodies of the cattle. A large cloud had covered the moon and the kerosene lamp only lit their immediate surroundings, casting a feeble amber circle around his feet.

He put a finger over his mouth. It wouldn't do to disturb the animals. They'd get flighty and likely crush some of the calves in their panic. He signaled to Matthew that he'd sneak around the one edge of the fencing and that Matthew should go around the long way. Matthew paused for a moment, clearly concerned about letting Kenan go off alone, but then his jaw tightened as he made a decision and he disappeared around the corner.

Kenan waited until he was sure that he was alone, then he crept toward the noise that was becoming louder by the second.

As he approached, he realized that it sounded like the whimpering of a child and his stomach flipped. What would an infant be doing out here at night? But then the clouds cleared, exposing the moon in all of her brilliant glory, and he could make out a shape huddled behind the fencing.

It was too big to be a child.

It was William Montgomery.

Kenan crept closer until he was right next to the figure and only the fencing lay between them.

"Mr Montgomery?"

The figure started but continued to snivel.

"William?" Kenan tried again. "Is that you?"

Kenan lifted the lamp so that the glow fell over the man's bulk. He was crouching against the fence, his arms wrapped tightly around his legs and his head pressed into his knees. His whole body quivered with terror.

Kenan reached through the fence and poked the man's leg.

"Arghh!" William Montgomery yelped then raised his tear soaked face to seek out his torturer. "Who are you? Whadda ya want?"

"Hush!" Kenan snapped. "You'll set the whole damned herd upon ya! It's me...Kenan Duggan."

William frowned at Kenan but his expression showed no recognition.

"Leave me alone! Please!" His voice cracked and he buried his head again.

Kenan glared at him then looked around. He was alone with old Montgomery. The man's life lay in his hands. His heart beat quickened and raw fury swept through his body like ten thousand red ants. It plundered beneath his skin, crawled through his veins and poisoned his rational mind. Here, before him, was the man who had robbed him of his life, stolen the woman he loved and denied him his chance of happiness.

The land beyond the fencing seemed to call out to him. This was a wilderness. Though man could try to tame it, fence it in, build upon its surface, it would always be wild. That was what the Indians knew but the white men had failed to grasp. A man could work with the land, nurture the land, and even live upon the land, but he would never, ever destroy her feral origins. Out here, a fella could still obey his most primitive instincts and surrender to his baser urges for retribution.

Far off in the untamed darkness, a coyote called and another one answered, as if privy to Kenan's dark musings.

He gently released his gun from its holster then held it against his stomach.

"Mr Montgomery?"

The man stopped whimpering then looked up at Kenan.

"Get up to your feet."

The old man peered around as if suddenly confused.

"Where am I? How did I get here?"

"It's okay," Kenan muttered through gritted teeth.

As the man rose, Kenan took a step back, assaulted by the stink of human shit.

"What in the hell?"

"Oh." William looked down at himself. "Seems I had an accident." He pulled at his trouser legs then stared at his damp fingers.

Kenan shook his head. What was going on here? William Montgomery had soiled himself. The man was a wreck. Dammit! He wanted to get answers from Catherine's uncle, to find out why he had sold his niece to save his own skin.

"Stop fiddling with that!" Kenan was repulsed by the old man's attempts to shake out his pants. "Raise your hands."

"What?" William gazed at Kenan. "But why?"

"Because you are a dirty varmint and I'm gonna destroy ya..."

Kenan raised his gun and pointed it directly at Montgomery's heart.

The old man began to cry again. "But whadda I done? I don't know how I got here, sir. I'm lost."

"You been lost for a while, you bastard!" Kenan spat.

Voices sounded a ways off. Small circles of light moved across the land as the other men approached. Hell. They'd be here soon and his chance would be gone.

He lowered the lamp to the ground then held his gun out in front of him, supporting his one hand with the other. He found the trigger with one trembling finger. He looked into William Montgomery's eyes. The old man stared back and sudden understanding filled his face like the first rays of dawn.

"I've done something bad, ain't I?"

Kenan scowled at him. He tried to swallow but his mouth was bone dry.

"I did somethin' and it hurt ya...and yours?"

"That's right."

William hung his head. "Then I'm sorry, sir. I'm so, so sorry. I ain't been right. I'm sick and I don't know why! I can't..." He rubbed his eyes with a dirty hand. "I just can't remember anything like I used ta."

Kenan kept his pistol in position but he felt the ball of anger in his stomach begin to unfurl. William Montgomery had done wrong. He had failed as a man, as an uncle and as a human being. He had let another man take his niece to use her for his own pleasure. Catherine had been used and abused, physically and emotionally scarred. But this man before him had clearly paid for his crimes. Though Kenan knew that shooting Montgomery would provide a moment of satisfaction, he also knew that it would be fleeting. The man once known as William Montgomery had long since gone and left in his wake a weakened and childlike wreck. This remnant of a man was no danger to anyone and it seemed that this sickness of the mind was suffering enough.

Kenan holstered his gun then sighed with relief as the fiery ants scuttled out of his heated brain, trickled down his body and legs and ran off into the night.

"Kenan!" Matthew appeared at his side. "You found him!"

Kenan turned to his brother, wrapped an arm around his shoulders, then pulled him to his side. His throat ached with emotion. As the other men arrived and gingerly took hold of William Montgomery, all of them reluctant to touch him because of the shit stink, Matthew guided Kenan away.

"Come on, big brother. Let's get on home."

Kenan allowed himself to be led.

As they neared the house, he stopped and placed a hand upon Matthew's shoulder then looked into his eyes.

"You were there all along weren't ya?"

Matthew offered a weak smile.

"You saw what...what I was gonna do?"

"Kenan," Matthew spoke softly, his eyes full of love and concern. "You were gonna do what every man worth his salt would do. But I know why you didn't. And you're an even better man because of it."

Then Matthew pulled him into a rough, brotherly hug.

Matthew was right. It was time to go home.

Chapter Ten

Kenan awoke in the gray light of dawn. Groggy with sleep, he smiled as he recalled their nocturnal activities. When they'd got home last night, Catherine had snuck in after Rosie had fallen asleep and they'd made slow, tender love. He'd stirred once, about an hour ago, to find his cock rock hard and deeply immersed in Catherine's mouth. He'd reached out to pull her up to his chest but she'd stayed where she was and moved her lips and hands on him. The combination of her hot breath, the ridges on the roof of her mouth and the grazing of her teeth against his shaft had combined until he'd been unable to control himself and he'd come hard into her, shooting his seed deep into her throat. She'd swallowed his essence with pleasure then crawled up the length of his body and curled herself around him, her little head upon his shoulder.

He'd held her close for a while then been unable to resist any longer. Her warmth and her sweet scent had aroused him again, so he'd slipped his arm from beneath her and wriggled down the bed to return the favor. She'd gasped when he'd covered her cunny with his mouth and he'd run his tongue over her lips, before opening them with his fingers and seeking out her hard bud. He'd licked it and suckled it until she'd arched her back and cried out then he'd drunk deeply of her hot juices as she'd come against his mouth. Not wanting to waste her musky lubrication, he'd snuggled up behind her and slipped into her then she'd squeezed him with her pussy and he'd pulsed slowly into her whilst using his fingers to make her climax again.

But she was gone now. He rubbed his eyes. A chill settled in his belly as ideas began to nag at him but he tried to push them away. It was all okay now. He'd settled his score with old Montgomery and no longer had to seek out the old man for revenge. He hadn't forgotten about Thomas Henderson but that would keep for another day. All he wanted now was to move on and start to live his life again—to believe that it would all be okay.

A horse whinnied out in the barn and Kenan sat up straight. Which one of his brothers would be taking one of the horses out this early?

He jumped out of bed and pulled on his trousers, not bothering to put on his union suit first. The seams of the pants rubbed at his naked flesh and his cock felt unwontedly free as it swung against the itchy wool.

The barn door creaked. What in the hell…

He ran from the bedroom, through the living area and flung open the front door.

Suddenly, Catherine came into view, mounted on his horse. She was wearing her green traveling suit and she had a bundle tied to her back.

"Catherine!" he called. "What the hell are you doing?"

She looked at him over her shoulder then turned the horse around so that she could face him and mouthed *I'm sorry*. Her emerald eyes glistened with tears and her hair blazed crimson in the rising sun. She was more beautiful than ever and Kenan watched, his heart filled with confusion and awe, as she dug her heels into his mare's flanks then galloped away.

He walked out to the perimeter fence, oblivious to the stones that bruised his naked feet, and watched as her figure became smaller then disappeared from view.

Catherine rode hard. She knew that if she slowed down or even stopped that she would turn around and ride back to Kenan. Her heart felt fit to burst and her head was tight with pain. Kenan had looked so lost as he'd stood there watching her go. Though it hurt to do it, and she felt like she would die with the agony of being separated from him, she knew that it was for the best. The comments she'd overheard last night and her uncle's fragile state meant that she really had no choice. How could she stay with Kenan knowing that, in spite of their intense passion, he might never be able to forgive and forget what had happened? The words he had uttered on his return from the cattle trail just kept spinning round and round in her head like an incessant twister: *I'll not have folks saying that the Duggans have a harlot at their homestead*. Add to this the fact that her presence there could put Rosie's happiness in jeopardy and she felt compelled to leave.

And she was needed now, anyway, by her own relatives. Though something deep in her heart called out to her, reminding her that Edie and William had hurt her, let her walk into a life of shame and pain, she still felt the pull of familial obligation that she'd been brought up to believe in. Letting go of it was unthinkable. If she didn't have that, and she didn't have Kenan, what did she have? At least duty gave her something solid to cling to.

So she returned with a heavy heart and mind to the homestead of William and Edie Montgomery, not knowing what to expect when she got there, or if she was really even wanted.

Kenan stood in the yard watching the dust roused by Catherine's flight as it began to settle. He couldn't believe that she'd just taken his horse and ridden away. What on earth was wrong with her? Just hours ago she'd shown him her adoration through a very intimate act and now she had galloped away like the devil himself was on her tail without so much as a goodbye, let alone an explanation.

Had he done something to upset her? Had he said something in his sleep or even last night? She had been very quiet on their return from the wedding party but he'd suspected that she was tired and content to rest in his arms as they shared his saddle.

Following his encounter with Catherine's uncle, Kenan had felt the knot between his shoulder blades loosen and he could even believe that maybe it was okay to hope that there was the possibility of a normal life on the horizon. Perhaps he could move on, settle down and reclaim the dreams he'd once believed destroyed.

But now this. Had she changed her mind following the wedding? Did she believe that they could never have the happiness displayed last night by the bride and groom? Did she feel too damaged by events to look into the future? How he wished that he knew.

There was only one way to find out. He'd have to go after her.

* * * *

Kenan's heart beat in time with the hooves of Matthew's horse as it cantered across the plains. He knew he was taking a risk crossing Indian territory alone but he didn't care. He had to get to Catherine and quickly. He'd thrown his clothes on and briefly explained where he was going to his siblings then he'd saddled the horse and set off. He had a good idea about where Catherine was headed and he intended to try there first.

He made it across the windswept open space without any encounters then headed straight for the Montgomery homestead.

As he approached, the rickety wooden house looked deserted on its small plot of land. The immediate garden surrounding the house was overgrown and weeds tangled with the vegetables, choking the life from them in the same way that William Montgomery's illness was choking the sense from his mind. Kenan realized that Edie had a fulltime job caring for her husband and that chores such as cultivating produce to eat and sell had clearly had to take a back seat in the wagon. Unexpected pity washed over him as he wondered how they were managing to survive. Edie had never been that practical, being inclined to enjoy pampering more suited to a lady of breeding, and William had catered to her for the majority of their married life. No wonder she was taking it so hard now that her provider had failed in his primary role.

The wind howled around the house as if irritated by its presence on the otherwise flat open landscape and the morning sun cast the western side in shadows. The curtains at the front remained closed and Kenan wondered if he'd made a mistake. Perhaps Catherine hadn't come here. Maybe her heart was too raw at her uncle's betrayal and she couldn't face seeing him again. But that didn't sound like the Catherine he knew. She had far too good and honest a heart to turn her back on what she would see as her obligations.

He jumped from the saddle and tethered his horse to the fence at the front of the property. The mare snorted and a whinny from the adjacent barn told him that his horse was here too. He'd know that sound anywhere. He climbed the steps to the front porch then stood before the battered wooden planks of the door.

Memories assaulted him like an opponent raining blows upon him in a fistfight. Each one took his breath away and caused his heart to throb with pain. He closed his eyes in a futile attempt to shut them out but they played on, one after another — Catherine, adorned in green satin, stood just there by the fence in the rain, crimson hair falling over her shoulders, face red with cold and embarrassment, her traveling bag in a puddle at her feet. Catherine, dancing and laughing across the grass in front of the house, her feet and head bare, her skirts gathered up as she demonstrated an Irish jig. Catherine...

He put a hand out to steady himself and dug his fingertips into the rough wood in front of him. Catherine had reappeared in his life like a dream, lifting his heart and raising his hopes. Without her, he *had* nothing. Without her, he *was* nothing.

He raised his hand then knocked.

The sound echoed through the empty house and he held his breath, listening for footsteps.

He waited.

After what seemed like hours, he was rewarded by the soft patter of female feet and the door swung wide open to reveal Edie Montgomery. She peered at him, her hair sticking out from beneath a greying mop cap, her face ashen with exhaustion and concern.

"Mr Duggan," she croaked. "I didn't think we'd be seeing you again so soon."

Kenan removed his hat.

"How's Mr Montgomery?"

"How'd you think?" she huffed. "You saw the state on him last night, didn't ya? He ain't no good to man nor beast."

"Yes, ma'am, and it's mighty cruel when nature robs a man of his senses," he replied, biting back the question he was burning to ask.

"Anyways" — Edie Montgomery eyed his hastily clad frame — "I doubt you're here to ask after my husband."

Kenan didn't deny it. He stood and looked her straight in the eye.

"Catherine!" The old woman called over her shoulder.

A noise from within made Kenan lean to the side to look over Edie's shoulder. Catherine appeared from the dark depths of the house and Edie moved aside to allow her to pass. She walked out onto the porch, wiping damp hands on a stained apron tied at her waist.

He crushed his hat between his hands.

"It's okay," Catherine spoke softly to her aunt then pointed back into the house. "He's sleeping now."

Edie nodded then scowled at Kenan. "She's returned to help and I won't appreciate you taking her away again." She raised a hand to her brow where she wiped it dramatically to make a show of exhaustion. "We need her here. I can't...I can't manage alone."

Catherine squeezed her aunt's shoulder. The woman gave Kenan one more sweeping glance before turning and going inside then slamming the door behind her.

Catherine sat on the stoop and patted the space next to her.

"You knew I'd come here?"

"Of course." He sat next to her so that his thigh brushed hers.

"I'm so sorry, Kenan, for everything that's happened. I wish that it could have been different."

"Whoa!" He held up his hands. "Why are you apologizing? What's going on here, Catherine? I believed that we were trying to rebuild something between us. What happened?"

Catherine smoothed the apron out over her knees as if trying to iron out the creases. Kenan reached out and placed a hand over one of hers.

"Kenan." She snatched her hand away. "Please...please don't. Whenever you're near and whenever you touch me, I lose my will to do what's right. I just love you so much that it takes my breath away!" She raised tear-filled eyes to meet his. "But this just can't be now. Don't you see that?"

He frowned, then shook his head. "No...no I don't. I have to admit that I was shocked when I first saw you and it took me a while to adjust to what'd happened. I mean, I was mad that you left willingly but, hell, Catherine...it don't make no difference to me now. All I know is that I want you — body, mind and soul — and I can't see how I'm gonna make it through the rest of my life without you."

Catherine wiped her eyes with the edge of the apron then pushed her hair behind her ears.

"I know that it feels real bad right now but we have to be realistic here. We're not innocent young lovers anymore. Too much has happened. You might grow to resent me because of what I did and I couldn't bear that. I'd rather remember how good it was between us and how wonderful it's been these past few days. I'll not drag you and yours down with me into the mire. I'm ruined, Kenan. Like you said…I'm no better than a harlot."

Kenan threw his hat to the floor at his feet, causing dust to fly up into the air from the well-worn ground in front of the step.

"No, Catherine! No! I was mad when I said that. I didn't know what you'd been through. I didn't know how bad things were for you or I'd never have said that, I swear it!"

She shook her head. "You believe that now but…"

He reached out for her hand again.

"But what?"

"In time…you might find that it grows and chokes you, poisons your feelings for me like a tainted Indian arrow."

"No!" he exclaimed, bile burning his throat like raw moonshine.

He looked at her carefully, realization dawning on him.

"Someone said something. Last night?"

Catherine turned away, staring out at the golden grass as it waved and swished in the breeze. The rising sun gave it a warm glow so that it looked like the land was coated in thick liquid gold.

"What was said, sweetheart?" He raised her hand and kissed it. Her skin was hot, as if she burned with the knowledge that she held inside.

"It doesn't matter," she whispered. "It makes no difference."

"Catherine..." His emotions rose in his throat, threatening to choke him. "Of course it does. Now tell me."

"When..." She ran the fingers of her free hand through her hair, pushing its heavy waves back from her face. As the breeze blew the tendrils back into her eyes, she smiled absently. "When you left last night, to look for my uncle...I went inside with Rosie. We sat quietly for a while and she told me about her..." She glanced at him and he realized that she was unsure how much he knew about Rosie's budding relationship with Joshua Hampton.

"It's okay, Catherine." He smiled. "Joshua has already spoken to me about his feelings for Rosie."

"Well, as she spoke, I realized how pure and untainted their love is. Rosie has a flawless past and Joshua, well, he's a man."

"He's a bit younger than Rosie."

"Yes, I know that but it just doesn't matter, does it? They're in love and they want to be together."

"And so do we." He squeezed her hand.

"But Rosie and Joshua are lucky. They don't have anything standing in their way." She stared into his eyes and he watched as hers misted over, their clear green turning to hazy malachite.

"What's standing in our way, Catherine?"

"Everything that's happened. It wouldn't just affect us, Kenan. It would affect everyone—Rosie, Matthew, Emmett. If you took me to wife...which I don't know if you were planning to do...after...after all that's happened...but if you did, or even if you just let me stay on with you, then folks would talk. It would ruin the Duggan name and reputation."

Kenan frowned. She was right, of course she was, but he had only considered how it would affect him and Catherine. He hadn't really thought past their relationship. But his family were decent people and they only wanted the best for him. And that meant Catherine. Didn't it?

"It wouldn't matter to any of them, Catherine. They care about you too and they wouldn't give a damn about what folks said. We Duggans...we're a tough lot!"

Catherine's face blanched. "Yes, I know that Kenan but Rosie is in love. For real! She wouldn't be happy if she lost Joshua because of me and my tarnished name as an Indian whore!"

"Catherine!" He shook his head.

"I'm right, Kenan and you know I am. Just last night I heard Mr Hampton talking to one of the wedding guests." Her cheeks filled suddenly with color, like a flower unfolding before the sun.

"And what did he say?"

"The woman, I think she was a cousin of his, she said...she asked...if I was the woman who'd returned from her Indian abduction."

"We can put that right, Catherine. We can explain." He held his hands out to her, palms facing the sky.

"Explain what, Kenan? What is worse? The idea that I was an Indian whore, or that, in fact, I went to live in New York with a man I hadn't married and all because my uncle got himself into debt and sold me like a soiled dove?"

Kenan felt the muscle begin to twitch again in his jaw. His heart picked up speed and the red mist swirled around his ankles. The man in New York. That scoundrel Thomas Henderson! He'd gotten away with his mistreatment of Catherine and had probably moved on to some other poor young woman. Men like that just went around ruining folks' lives and taking what they wanted from whomever they chose. Well, it would have to stop.

"Catherine." Kenan took her hands in both of his. "It makes no difference to me and I don't give a damn what folks say. We'll not stoop to try to explain events to others. Damn them all to hell!"

"It won't work, Kenan. Mr Hampton told his guest that yes, I was the Indian whore but that I'd just been hired as Rosie's help at the homestead. He denied all knowledge of you and me being connected and said…" Her voice broke and she choked on a sob. "He said that if he suspected for a moment that you and I were…involved again, then he'd be sure to cut all ties between Rosie and Joshua."

Kenan felt his eyes widen as he struggled to comprehend what Catherine was telling him. "No." He shook his head. "No, he wouldn't do that. He wouldn't say that."

"He already has," Catherine murmured, tears now brimming in her eyes and trickling down her cheeks like tiny diamonds.

Kenan reached out and pulled her to his chest, pressing his face into her hair and wondering what in the hell he was going to do to put this all right.

Catherine allowed Kenan to hold her while she sobbed. When she finally tired and her tears dried up, she wiped her face on her apron then lifted her head.

"I'm sorry. That didn't help at all." She attempted a smile.

"Well, no but I know how you're feeling," Kenan replied, giving her chin a gentle squeeze.

She patted around her eyes with her forefingers, gently feeling the swollen flesh. It was ironic that when she'd returned from New York, she'd believed that her days of heartbreak were finally over. In fact, it seemed that they were really just beginning. Now she would be close enough to see Kenan on a regular basis, yet unable to be with him in the way that she wished.

"It's been so good seeing you again." She was suddenly embarrassed about what a mess she must look wearing one of her aunt's old dresses and a tatty apron with her hair all loose and tangled from her horse ride.

"Catherine." He sighed, shaking his head. "You really have no idea, do you?"

"About what?" Her heart upped its pace.

"How I feel about you." He turned her head to face him then cupped her cheeks. His hands were warm and strong, hard and calloused against her soft skin. Heat and hope stirred in her belly.

"But it makes no difference," she said, willing him to deny it. "I cannot jeopardize Rosie's happiness, I cannot place you in a position where you may well resent my presence and..." Her stomach clenched. "And...I cannot forsake my uncle and aunt when they need me so much."

Kenan stared hard at her and she felt that she would lose herself in his chocolate brown eyes. His black eyebrows danced above them as a myriad of emotions passed over his face. For a moment, panic rose in her breast as he seemed to withdraw, his eyes closing against her, but it was over as soon as it had begun and his gaze filled once more with warmth and adoration.

"I have an idea. Well, two actually." His face lit up with a grin, causing the corners of his eyes to crinkle.

Catherine fought against the ray of hope that flickered in her belly, terrified of acknowledging it in case she had to extinguish it again.

"Firstly, I'm going to go talk to Joshua. He truly loves Rosie. I'd bet my last dime on it and I doubt that he'd let his old man ruin it all for him. A good woman's hard to find and my twin sister is as good as they come. Present company excepted, of course!"

Catherine's lips twitched at the corners in spite of her determination to maintain a solemn air of dignity. It would protect her from the disappointment that would so surely come. She must not allow it to slip.

"But Kenan...Mr Hampton sounded so determined last night. He'll not allow it, I'm sure of it."

"It's not his decision to make who we Duggans allow into our lives. As for Joshua...he respects his ol' man but I've seen the way he looks at Rosie and I'm sure he'd go through hell and high water to be with her."

Catherine dug her nails into her palms. Could she dare to hope?

"And secondly..." Kenan leaned over and picked up his hat, then absently brushed the dust from it. "I'm going to find your aunt some help. I'll employ someone to give her a hand around here with the running of the place and with the care of Mr Campbell. That way, Edie can't go complaining or making you feel guilty no more!"

Catherine felt her face straining as a grin emerged. She couldn't help it. She'd come here this morning, expecting to tie herself down to a life of drudgery and denial with her father's brother and his wife and instead, the man she'd loved had arrived like a knight in a fairy-tale on an almost white horse, then offered her a solution to her problems. It was just too good to be true.

But then she felt the familiar sinking of her heart as her final fear spoke up. What about Kenan's feelings for her? How could he really want her as his wife, as his lifelong partner, as the mother of his children when she'd been used as a whore by another man?

"Kenan..." She stood and smoothed out her skirts. "There was the...the other thing too..."

He looked up into her face then placed his hat on the step beside him. When he took her hands in his and held them to his lips, she felt like her heart would burst. Since her return, her love for him had grown, matured, developed and it now ran like sweet, warm honey through her veins. In just a matter of days, she had confirmed what she already knew. She loved this man with everything that she was, and losing him again would break her heart into a thousand pieces, just like falling from a wild stallion would break her body. Though she knew she'd face the latter fate a thousand times over if she could just be with Kenan again.

"Catherine," he breathed.

"Yes, my love."

"We cannot change what has happened. We cannot go back in time to be the people that we once were."

She shook her head and bit her lower lip to still its trembling. How cruel life was — how unjust and unfair!

"But Catherine...my life without you...thinking that you were gone forever...was unbearable."

"I am so sorry!" The tears began to flow from her tender eyes once more.

"But..." Now Kenan's voice broke. "I...I know now that you live and I am so, so thankful for it. I swear to you Catherine, that if you will have me...if you will take me as your husband and be by my side each day until we breathe our last... I swear to you that I will never let you down. I will protect you, honor you and love you with every part of me."

Catherine swallowed hard. Her head swam with emotion and she had to slow down her breathing. What was he saying? Did he really mean it?

"Well, darn it, girl!" Edie Montgomery's voice snapped at her from the front door. "What in the hell are ya waiting for? A chorus of God's own angels to serenade ya whilst ye make up ya mind? Take him up on it now or I'll beat ya to it!"

Catherine stared at her aunt, surprise and joy battling deep inside.

She started to laugh through her tears.

"Oh, Kenan, yes! Yes. Yes. A thousand times yes.

She pulled at his hands to bring him to his feet then fell into his arms and relaxed into the warmth and the passion of his kiss.

* * * *

Catherine walked onto the front step of the Duggan homestead. She placed her hands on the smooth wood of the porch rail and savored the warmth of the wood. Throughout the course of the day, the sun had warmed it as it did the front step. Kenan's father had been a talented man and craftsmanship meant that the place was a real home.

The autumnal evening sky glowed red and amber. She closed her eyes, savoring the fading warmth of the setting sun.

Horse hooves alerted her to the return of her husband and she skipped off the step and ran to the perimeter fence, her heart beating with joy at the idea of being in his arms again, though he'd only been gone half a day into Virginia City to fetch supplies. Not far behind him, she could make out the wagon as it trundled along with Emmett wobbling on the wooden plank that served as a seat.

Kenan leaped from his mare then tethered her before gathering Catherine carefully into his arms.

"Kenan!" She laughed. "You don't need to be so gentle with me! I'm not going to break!"

He kissed her on the mouth, the chin, the forehead and both cheeks before leaning over and planting a tender kiss upon her belly.

"How did it go in town?" Catherine asked as he wrapped an arm around her shoulders.

"All sorted. I think I got everything you asked for." He rolled his eyes.

She mock punched him in the chest.

"Any news?" She traced the frown that passed over his forehead with her forefinger. "What is it?"

"Not a lot's happening in Virginia City. Same old same old..." He shrugged but Catherine could sense his unease.

"Has someone said something about...about me?" She heard the quiver in her own voice and felt the familiar surge of fear. Was it possible that someone, somewhere, could even now—more than three months after her reunion with Kenan—destroy her happiness?

"I didn't know whether to tell you but I can't hide it from you either." He caressed her cheeks then planted a soft kiss upon her nose.

"Please...what is it?"

"I spoke to the sheriff earlier. He'd just received some news from New York City."

"Oh!" Catherine's heart thrummed like a caged bird and she felt the ever present nausea threaten.

"It's not nice to hear, mind."

She lifted her chin, steeling herself. "Please tell me."

"Seems that Thomas Henderson..." She watched as the small muscle at the corner of Kenan's jaw began to twitch again. She knew how thinking of that man made Kenan's blood boil still and she guessed that it always would.

"Yes?" She placed a trembling hand upon Kenan's chest.

"Seems he got himself into a bit of a tricky situation."

"What did he do?" She gripped his shirt front.

"He tried to take himself another man's fiancée...just like he took you."

She felt her mouth fall open and she searched his eyes wildly, fearing yet longing to hear the rest.

"And what happened?"

"He got caught out this time. The young woman went along with it all to pay off her father's debts but her fiancé found out where she'd gone and—"

"Oh no!" Catherine's hand flew up to her mouth.

"Yep!" Kenan licked his lips. "Now...I promised you I'd not go after retribution and I kept my promise but it seems like Henderson got what was comin' to him."

Catherine leaned forwards and rested her head on his chest. She breathed deeply of his familiar scent and focused on slowing her heartbeat. So Thomas Henderson was dead. He'd hurt her and the man she loved then he'd tried to do the same again. Who knew how many times he'd succeeded in the past? Maybe Catherine hadn't been the first. In fact, she sincerely doubted that she had.

When she had mastered her emotions and felt long awaited relief seeping through her like a refreshing breeze in high summer, she spoke again.

"So despite the fact that we still live in a relatively untamed land…" Catherine spread her arms out, gesturing at the plains surrounding the homestead. "It seems that folks can't just go around acting any old way they want."

"No sweetheart," Kenan pulled her into his embrace. "They really can't."

"I love you, Kenan. I love you so much and I'm so happy to be here with you."

"And I'm the happiest man alive…" He turned her so that her back rested against his chest and stomach and he wrapped his arms around her. "Now that I know I can come home to my wife" — he placed a protective hand over her stomach and cupped the slight curve — "and my growing child."

Catherine covered his hand with her own and relaxed against her husband's warmth, secure in the knowledge that for them, at least, life would go on as they had originally planned at the Duggan homestead.

A RANCHER
FOR ROSIE

Dedication

For my own family, who are my world.
XXX

Chapter One

"Oh Rosie...it hurts so much."

Catherine's clenched teeth and ashen face made Rosie's stomach churn. She had never helped a woman in labor before and she didn't have any personal experience to draw upon.

Though at my age a woman would hope to have delivered a few babes of her own.

She shook her head. No sense dwelling on that now. She had a job to do. She had to help her sister-in-law through this.

"Rosie, I'm certain it's too soon. I thought the little one wasn't due until April."

Rosie placed a hand on Catherine's shoulder. "I'm sure it will be fine. The whore I spoke with in town told me that sometimes a woman can get her dates muddled and sometimes a babe is ready earlier than expected."

Rosie's cheeks grew hot as Catherine stared hard at her. Catherine was no fool, and Rosie knew that her twin brother's wife could see right through her attempts at reassurance. But Rosie could also sense Catherine's desire to be comforted and her need to be supported in the absence of her husband or a more qualified birthing partner.

Right now, Rosie was all Catherine had.

Poor girl!

Rosie fluttered like a nervous butterfly as Catherine shuffled around the small homestead. Catherine had stripped down to her shift as her body had overheated with the pains that had increased in intensity by the hour. At intervals, she grabbed the nearest piece of furniture and held on tightly as she rode the waves that shook her petite frame. Rosie trembled along with Catherine as the laboring woman's knuckles grew white with the force of her grip on table edge or bench. The color only returned to Catherine's skin when the agony receded. But Rosie had learned quickly that the routine would begin all over again. Soon. And she could do nothing to help.

She longed to rush out to the stable, saddle a horse and gallop straight into town to find Matthew but she feared leaving Catherine alone. What if something happened while she was gone? *But what if something happens while you tarry here afraid?*

Oh, Matthew, hurry up with help!

And, Joshua, please bring Kenan home soon.

Joshua—sweet, handsome Joshua Hampton, who had the power to lift Rosie's heart up to the clouds. Just the thought of his handsome face with its bright blue eyes and full, sensual mouth made her heart beat faster. The thought of running her hands though his thick, sandy blond hair as he pressed his lips to hers made her body tighten in a way she had never experienced before their first embrace. He made Rosie feel beautiful, desirable and safe. And she wished with all of her heart that he was here.

"Come now, Catherine. Why don't you lie down? This could take a while and you should rest. You need to save your strength."

Catherine nodded and waddled toward the rear of the house. She opened the door that led to a short corridor and four bedrooms then went into her own. Rosie helped her to climb onto the bed and tucked the blankets around her.

"Try to sleep now, Catherine."

Catherine eased herself out of the blankets. "I'm too warm to lie beneath these and I doubt that the pains will allow me to sleep, Rosie."

"I know, dear heart, but you must try. At least rest between them. I'm sure that Matthew will be back soon."

Catherine offered a wan smile before closing her eyes and sinking into the feather-stuffed pillow.

Rosie paused for a moment, wondering whether to take the chair in the corner of the room. But she realized that her presence might disturb Catherine, so she decided she would leave the doors ajar and listen instead. She tiptoed out of the room and headed back into the kitchen area, where she slumped into a fireside chair.

Matthew had headed out at first light when it seemed that the pains afflicting Catherine were not false signs of labor—as they had hoped—but real ones. It was now almost four in the afternoon. *Where is he?* Rosie's shoulders ached with tension, her head hurt from worrying and her heart ached for another reason.

She leaned forward and rested her forehead on her arms.

Will Joshua ever ask me to marry him?

It had been months since he had first shown an interest in her. Months since she had been stunned by his attention — attention that went beyond that of good manners toward the sister of a friend. At first, Joshua had been extremely shy. Painfully so. Considering how handsome he was and the fact that he exuded raw masculinity, his shyness had endeared him to Rosie even more. She had wondered initially if he saw her only as Kenan's sister, as a woman too old to consider romantically, and had treated him kindly as she would any family friend. But gradually, his awkwardness around her had eased and they had become friends, talking for hours about the people they knew and the places he had seen during his time on the cattle trails.

They had kissed and shared several more intimate moments. Joshua had whispered promises of what he would soon say and do, of how happy they would be. After all, what was the appropriate time for a courtship? She knew Joshua's reasons for his delay in actually proposing, and they were sensible enough. Respectable enough. Joshua had a lot of responsibility on his shoulders and he couldn't just up and leave the family business. He also wanted to be able to provide for Rosie himself, not just offer her all that he possessed as the son of a successful rancher. So he was saving his wages from his time on the cattle trail in order to build them a home of their own. She should've been glad that he was not impetuous and carried away on a wave of passion that could have ruined them both. But it didn't extinguish the flames of her desire for him, and it didn't help her to curb her own impatience which reared its ugly, vulnerable head during the darkest hours of the night.

Mayhap she was a fool to be ruled by her heart and her desire. She had seen Kenan's brow furrow several times when Joshua had stayed for supper, as if he was trying to work out exactly what Joshua wanted from Rosie. But Kenan also held Joshua in high esteem. Surely, if he doubted him for a second, he would put an immediate stop to his visits to the Duggan homestead? So she should continue to show trust. To believe. To wait.

What else could a woman do?

She sat up and shrugged. Here she was fretting over a man when her poor sister-in-law was about to deliver the first baby the old homestead had seen in over twenty years. What a gift this child would be. A new generation. A new hope. A new start for Catherine and Kenan.

And a painfully stark reminder of Rosie's own childless state.

* * * *

"Rosie!"

The cry pierced through the fog in Rosie's mind.

"Rosie...please..."

Again.

Rosie lifted her head from her arms. Shadows loomed in the homestead with the onset of evening. The corners of the room were filled with darkness and she shivered with the fleeting memory of an unpleasant dream. She had fallen asleep. *For how long?*

She rubbed her eyes then stood.

"Catherine?"

No answer. Her voice seemed to be swallowed by the eerie emptiness of the homestead. Without her brothers, it was as hollow as an abandoned mineshaft. She rubbed her upper arms briskly.

"I'm coming, Catherine." She held her breath but there was still no reply.

Something is wrong…

She hurried through to Catherine's bedroom and nearly dropped to the floor at the sight that greeted her.

Catherine was hunched over on the bed, her long hair damp and matted as it clung to her face. She rocked from side to side and moaned like a wounded animal. Her thin shift was no longer pure white but stained dark in places. In the fading light, Rosie could just make out that the stain was red. As were Catherine's hands and the bed sheet, and there was even a red pool on the floor.

"Dear Lord in heaven, Catherine!" Rosie's hands shook as she reached out to her sister-in-law and took hold of her shoulders. "How long have you been like this?"

"I…I woke up…about half an hour since…the pain is so bad now, Rosie. I'm so scared."

Rosie looked into Catherine's eyes and saw terror and despair. Catherine needed her right *now*. Though Rosie was overwhelmed by an urge to run from the room, screaming about the blood and the pain and the sweat and the unknown—she could not. She owed it to the woman she now held to her breast, to her brother whom she loved with a fierce devotion and to the tiny baby not yet born. She had to give them a fighting chance.

She took a kerosene lamp from its hook on the wall and lit it then hung it back up. It cast a yellow circle of light over the bed and the floor. It made her feel a bit better. Ridiculous, perhaps. But it banished the gathering shadows to the corners and lifted her spirits.

"Right, Catherine, let's get you cleaned up then I can see better how far along you are."

How far along? How the hell would you know?

Rosie filled the white china bowl on the dresser with fresh water from the matching jug and dipped a cloth into it. She had prepared a pile of rags and left them in Catherine's room in readiness. She wrung the cloth then took it over to Catherine. She wiped her hot cheeks, cleansed the blood from her hands then did the same to her feet. *So much blood.* And there was another fluid, some sort of murky water that poured from Catherine's insides like a flash flood every time she endured another contraction of her womb.

Did women really do this every day?

The whore she had consulted told her that they did. Lucky women had female relatives to consult when they went into labor, experienced women who could offer advice and support. Poor Catherine did not. She had Rosie. And as Rosie had known next to nothing about giving birth, she had been forced to seek out a soiled dove to question. The whore had tried to reassure Rosie that all would be well if she just kept Catherine calm, but now that it was actually happening, Rosie wasn't convinced. The pains that Catherine had endured seemed to be getting worse. The whore had also warned her that sometimes the bag holding the baby might burst, which explained the amount of fluid that Catherine was losing, but Rosie hadn't expected there to be *so much*. The bed was drenched and Rosie's waters dripped from the covers onto the wooden floorboards where it created an ever widening circle.

She needed to get Catherine out of her wet clothes and to dress the bed with fresh linen then try to clean the floor. At least she could do that.

"Can you stand, Catherine?"

"I...I'm not sure. Every time I move, the pains come." She gave a wry laugh. "Even when I don't move, they come."

Rosie wrapped an arm around Catherine's shoulder.

"I'll help you up and we'll take it slowly. Squeeze my hand if you need to."

Catherine's jaw tightened and Rosie realized that she was gritting her teeth. *Poor girl.* Though Catherine was but a few years her junior, Rosie felt protective of her. Catherine had been through a lot before she'd finally become Mrs. Duggan, and although Rosie didn't know the whole story, the scars on Catherine's arms told her enough. Catherine knew what it was to suffer, to be torn from the man she loved, and she deserved to be happy now.

Rosie braced herself as Catherine edged off the bed and hobbled to the chair in the corner of the room.

When Catherine was seated, Rosie hurriedly stripped the bed and tossed the soiled sheets aside. Luckily, the patchwork coverlet and cotton sheet had caught the worst of the fluids and the burlap ticking mattress was still dry underneath. She grabbed clean linen from the chest at the bottom of the bed and breathed deeply of the lavender fragrance. Soothing. Familiar. Safe. As always, the fresh scent brought a flood of memories of childhood, and images of her own dear mother. The older Mrs. Duggan would have known what to do. Rosie blinked away hot tears.

If only Mother was here. But she's not, so you need to be strong.

She tucked the sheet in at the corners then turned back to Catherine.

"Now for your shift."

Catherine lifted her arms and Rosie tugged the damp garment over her head. She swallowed a gasp at the sight of Catherine's naked body. It was remarkable. Swollen with child, she appeared full, fertile, female. Beautiful. As Rosie watched, Catherine gripped the seat of the chair and began to breathe heavily. Her belly seemed to tighten to a point at her protruding navel as she gulped for air. Just when it seemed that Catherine might actually burst and the babe come tumbling from her body, her panting slowed and her abdomen relaxed and returned to its former smooth roundness.

The pains were working their ancient, womanly magic and Rosie wondered if she would ever feel their power. Ever feel a child quicken in her own womb.

She dunked a clean cloth into the basin and washed Catherine quickly, before another pain set in. When she was happy that her sister-in-law was thoroughly cleansed, she pulled a clean shift from a dresser drawer and helped Catherine into it.

"Now back to bed with you."

Catherine nodded and allowed Rosie to help her.

"I'm real scared, Rosie. What if Kenan doesn't make it back and something goes wrong. What if I can't do this and I lose the babe?"

Rosie shook her head. "Nonsense, sweetheart. You can and will do this. It's not called labor for nothing, ya know. Hardest day's work of your life…so they say."

Catherine blanched and Rosie took her hands. It broke her heart to feel Catherine tremble with the effort of riding the agonizing waves. She would take the pain for her if she could. That was how much she cared for Catherine and her brother.

It was time to do what she had been dreading. To assess how far along Catherine was. The soiled dove had shown her how to feel inside a woman to check if the neck of the womb was open and ready to release the babe into the world. She had said that when the leg trembling began, it was a sign that the child was making its way out. But if this happened before the way was ready...then complications could follow.

"Lie back, Catherine. I need to see if you're ready to deliver."

"I think I feel like pushing, Rosie. I think...but I'm not sure... I'm so tired."

Rosie smoothed Catherine's red hair back from her forehead and smiled. "Well, let's see, shall we?"

She helped Catherine to lie back then rubbed her hands together. In spite of the perspiration on her brow and the damp beneath her armpits, Rosie's hands were freezing.

She placed her left knee on the bed and reached out for the hem of Catherine's shift. Taking a deep breath, she steeled herself, preparing to conduct an examination, the like of which she had only seen carried out on a horse, when she heard a shout from outside.

She jumped from the bed. She glanced at Catherine. Then at the open doorway.

Thank goodness!

Someone had come home. She smoothed out her skirts and tucked her hair back into its bun.

"I'll check who it is, Catherine. Stay as still as you can. Help is on the way."

Rosie rushed from the room and out through the homestead, her heart thudding. Was it Kenan and

Joshua? Had they come home just in time? Or was it Matthew returned from town with help?

She opened the door, a greeting of joy poised on her lips, then she let out a sigh of despair as she saw who had just arrived.

Chapter Two

Mr. Hampton tethered his horse to the rail in front of the porch then loped toward the house. Though his strides were tempered by his old injury, he exuded the easy confidence of a man of means.

Rosie's stomach somersaulted, and she battled the urge to slam the door and rush back into the house. She knew that Joshua's father wasn't pleased about the attention his son paid her, and she could understand why. At thirty-two, she was seven years older than the handsome cowboy. Joshua came from a well-to-do home, Mr. Hampton having created a prosperous cattle driving business, and they lived on an enormous ranch which he'd built from scratch. Rosie, however, lived at a modest homestead which had been built by her Irish father and was now the property of her twin brother, the eldest son. She had nothing to offer Joshua or his family.

Except for my love.

And when was that ever going to seem like enough to a businessman like Mr. Hampton?

He climbed the steps to the porch and approached her.

"Evening, Miss Duggan." He briefly lifted his Stetson in greeting. The shadow from the porch and the light behind him meant that Rosie was unable to see his eyes. It unnerved her.

"Evening, Mr. Hampton. Is everything all right?" Panic seized her as she wondered if something had happened to Kenan or Joshua. Had he come to tell her that they'd been hurt, or worse? The cattle trail could be a dangerous place, even for fit young men like her twin brother and Joshua.

"Yeah, yeah." He rubbed his chin with a large hand on which the blue veins stood out like bark on a tree trunk. Rosie noted that it trembled slightly. "I've not come to you with bad news. Well...at least I don't think it's bad news."

"Oh." She dug her fingernails into her palms. What did he want then? He'd never come out to the homestead before, and she hadn't ever spoken to him alone. If she was completely honest, he made her feel uneasy and self-conscious—on edge. It was a real shame, because she would have liked to feel a connection to the father of the man she adored, had hoped that he might see why Joshua held her in high esteem. But that reassurance seemed to elude her and it made her sad. She mentally shook herself. There was no point worrying over things she couldn't change, especially when Catherine was laboring away inside. She couldn't bear to be out here when her sister-in-law needed her.

"Listen, Miss Duggan, I'm not gonna string this out any more than I have to. I needed to straighten a few things up. You're a comely wench and all that..." He motioned at her figure, taking her in with a wave of his hand that moved from her head to her feet. It made her feel like a heifer being sized up for breeding. "But we both know that you're not a good long-term prospect for my son."

Rosie's palms instantly dampened, and she wiped them on her apron. "I...I'm sorry? I don't understand."

Mr. Hampton shifted then removed his hat. Rosie met eyes that had once clearly been as bright blue as Joshua's, but were now milky and diluted. What was it that stole their color and made them so hazy? Dylan Hampton was a handsome man, he was strong and broad-shouldered, in spite of his advancing years. But today, Rosie sensed a change in him, as if he was trying to maintain the façade of strength. As if he was refusing to give in to some physical ailment which plagued him.

"Now, now, Miss Duggan. I'm sure that you do. I know from what Joshua has said about you that you're no idiot."

No idiot! What?

Rosie bit her lip. Had he come here to provoke her then? To rouse her to indignation? And to what end?

"Mr. Hampton, much as I'd like to chew the fat with you, I can't be hanging around here all day. My sister-in-law is inside...in labor...and she needs me."

"You're alone?" He frowned.

Rosie inclined her head. "Matthew has gone into town to fetch help."

Mr. Hampton paused. "Well, I wish that sister-in-law of yours the best of luck. She'll need it, no doubt." His upper lip curled slightly as if with distaste.

Rosie bridled at his remark. So Dylan Hampton was still holding on to the image of Catherine as a harlot. His prejudice made her toes curl, but then he wasn't much different from most other folks.

After Catherine's arrival, it had taken a while for the rumors and the disdain to blow over. Yet here was the father of the man she loved, raking over old horse shit. Well, she'd be damned if she was going to stand here and listen to him.

"Well, goodbye, Mr. Hampton."

"Now wait a second, miss!" The harshness of his tone froze Rosie to the spot. "I've not finished what I came here to say."

"Then do so quickly, please, sir, as I need to be getting inside."

"To put it bluntly then... I want you to have no more to do with my son. Ya see, I think that this nonsense between you and Joshua has been going on long enough. It's time to put a stop to it. You have no place in his life and no welcome at our home. You're past your...your prime and he needs a young, healthy wife with a more suitable background. If you don't pay heed and you continue to encourage Joshua, then he may just end up disinherited."

The porch seemed to sway beneath Rosie's feet and she grasped at the post beside her. So Dylan Hampton had finally decided to put an end to her relationship with Joshua. She had been surprised that it hadn't happened before and had been lulled into a false sense of security by Mr. Hampton's lack of interference and Joshua's sweet attention. But now here it was, cold and harsh as winter winds.

How could I do that to him?

"I...I'm not sure..." *Quite how to respond...* Emotion welled in her throat and choked her. It was all she could do to suck in small, desperate breaths.

"Well, then. I've said what I came to say, so I'll be off." Dylan Hampton stared at her for a moment and she shook under his gaze. He lifted a hand as if to reach out to her then looked at it and dropped it to his side.

He stepped off the porch and untied his horse. Before mounting the beast, he paused and turned back to Rosie. "Miss Duggan, I don't mean to cause pain. Ya seem like a nice enough woman, but I just want more for Joshua. The best for my boy. You can understand that, surely?"

Of course she could understand that. Of course. Surely that what was every good parent wanted for their children...*the best*.

As Dylan Hampton settled into his saddle, pausing for a moment to adjust his gun belt, Rosie blinked away the stinging tears then turned and staggered back into the house, banishing the vision of the man who had just broken her heart.

Rosie shut the door behind her and leaned on it heavily, gasping for breath. Her chest hurt and she felt sure that she'd vomit. All of her hopes and dreams had just been crushed, and the future she had dared to envisage had been ripped away.

She could never marry Joshua. *Never.* Though she had, if she reached down into herself and dragged her deepest thoughts and feelings to the surface, never really believed that it would come to pass. Why would any man, let alone a handsome rancher's son, want to wed an old maid like her when he could choose any young female in the county? Joshua had prospects. Rosie had none.

"Rosie!"

Poor Catherine. Where on earth is Matthew?

She flung the door open and lurched onto the porch. She could make out Dylan Hampton riding away and someone approaching.

Two horses. Two figures. Their silhouettes were black against the horizon.

She squinted, but the dust kicked up by the horses made it impossible to see who it was. At least someone was on the way. She just hoped it was Matthew with help.

Rosie had barely begun to smooth Catherine's hair from her fevered brow when she heard feet on the porch and an agitated man's voice followed by a softer, calmer one. Was that a woman? Footsteps moved through the house and she looked up as Matthew filled the doorway.

"Oh, thank goodness! She's near the end and I've been so worried about trying to deliver the babe." Rosie's words of relief flooded the room and it was all she could do to maintain a hold on her emotions.

Matthew smiled as he stood aside and a young woman stepped past him. Rosie bit her lip and swallowed a gasp. The young woman he had brought to help Catherine was clearly of mixed race. She wore a plain navy blue housedress with her sleek black hair gathered into a knot at the nape of her neck. Her skin was clear and smooth and the color of coffee with cream. She was a combination of two worlds, a reminder of what had been and how it had changed because of the overbearing presence of the white man. And, she was one of the most beautiful young women that Rosie had ever seen.

The woman approached the bed and gestured at Catherine. "May I?" She kept her eyes lowered as if afraid of being presumptuous.

Rosie glanced at Catherine. "Yes, of course. Please do."

Rosie moved to Matthew's side. She frowned at him.

He shrugged. "What's wrong, Rosie?" he whispered, his eyes fixed on the face of the midwife.

"She's so young... I was expecting you to bring a...a whore. Someone older and more experienced."

Matthew threw her a curious glance. "She was recommended. It took me so long to get back because she was tending to another woman in town, so I had to wait until she was done. She's a Sioux midwife. No children herself apparently, but skilled in delivery and knowledgeable about female ailments, according to the woman she was working for."

"Working for?" Rosie queried.

"As a maid. Her employer said that she's reliable and quiet. No trouble. Just a good worker. She has helped deliver many babes in town and is in demand. Catherine's lucky to have her."

"Oh." It seemed that Matthew had done well. "Good." Rosie became aware that she was clenching her hands and pressed them into her skirts to still them. "Does she have a name?"

"Huyana."

Rosie stared at her brother. The way that he said the woman's name suggested admiration and respect. It tripped from his lips like a summer breeze through a willow tree. The way that he looked at her right now suggested... *Oh, Matthew.* He was intrigued by the maiden he'd just met. Matthew — who rarely talked of women or the future, who avoided social gatherings with a thousand excuses. He had never spoken of love or named a woman he admired. Yet here he was, clearly captivated. Rosie felt a flutter of pleasure and pride. Matthew, her younger brother, had finally seen a woman who could penetrate his cool veneer. Like Kenan, he knew his own mind and was strong and stubborn. Typical then that his woman of choice would be different—a woman whom some in society might frown upon. A beautiful Sioux maiden.

The flutter grew and spread to create a smile upon her lips. The Duggans would love whomever they would love and that was how it should be. Scars, skin tone, age, sin. None of them mattered in the face of true love.

"Time for you to leave." Rosie ushered Matthew from the room. "This is no place for a man."

Matthew nodded, but cast Huyana one more lingering glance before going. Yes, that was certainly the look of a man falling for a woman.

Rosie had seen it in Joshua's eyes.

Her heart sank.

But now, Mr. Hampton had won. And love, in Rosie's case, had lost.

Chapter Three

Rosie held Catherine's hand as she pushed her tiny, red baby into the world. Huyana had been wonderful throughout the final stages of the birth. The midwife was calm and organized. She coaxed and soothed Catherine every step of the way, barely blinking as Catherine squealed and panted in the most guttural, animal way. The thought that she would like the young woman at her side as she gave birth herself flittered through Rosie's mind, but it was quickly banished as she realized that she would probably never experience this female rite of passage.

Not now. Not anymore.

Huyana handed the baby to Rosie and she swaddled it in a clean white sheet, carefully wrapping the wriggling arms against the little body. Her hands trembled as she did so, betraying her own anxiety about hurting the new arrival.

While Huyana tended to Catherine, cleaning her efficiently and wordlessly, Rosie handed the wide-eyed infant to its mother.

Catherine's eyes filled with tears as she took her baby into her arms and held it to her breast.

"So beautiful," she whispered reverently, and Rosie was stunned by the pang of envy that pierced her. Catherine was so lucky to have a child. She longed to hold a baby of her own, but that would never happen. She would never know the joy of nursing a little girl or boy, of gazing into a newborn's eyes and knowing that she had created that child with the man she loved.

"She's perfect, Catherine." Rosie pushed through her own pain. She would not create a cloud over Catherine's joy. She loved her sister-in-law and believed that she deserved to be happy, especially after all that she had been through.

"She?" Catherine giggled and kissed the tiny head with its covering of downy red hair—red like Catherine's. Rosie wondered for a moment if it would stay that color or turn the ebony shade of Kenan's.

"What will you name her, Catherine?"

The new mother shook her head. "I'm not sure. Not yet. I'll wait for Kenan and we'll decide together."

"That's for the best," Rosie replied. "Don't want to fall out over a name." She smiled, knowing that Kenan would never disagree with Catherine's choice. He adored his wife and did everything in his power to make her happy. It would be so good to see Kenan's reaction when he arrived home and met his new daughter.

"Excuse me?" Huyana stood by the door with a basin full of bloodied cloths. "I will go wash these now that the lady is well."

"You will not!" Rosie admonished and she saw the young woman wince. What made her so anxious? She had just helped them in ways that they would never be able to fully thank her for. She had, without a doubt, saved Catherine and the little one. Rosie would have struggled to help them both through the final moments and her gratitude for all that Huyana had done swelled in her heart and threatened to burst forth in a torrent of tears and garbled words. "What I meant...Huyana...was that you have done enough here. We are so grateful for your assistance. I will wash the cloths."

"Oh..." Huyana lifted her big, brown eyes from the floor for a moment and Rosie saw the confusion within them. She had the air of someone who had lived her whole life subserviently, in fear, afraid of displeasing others. She was Sioux, or half-Sioux at least. Rosie had no personal experience of Indian people herself, but she had heard the stories of their ferocity and savagery. *Yes, Rosie, stories.* And this maiden, Huyana, evidently had a sweet, kind nature, and Rosie hated to see anyone browbeaten. "Well, would Mrs. Duggan like me to show her how to feed the child?"

Catherine reached out a hand to Huyana and waved her toward her side. "Please. I don't know where to start."

Rosie took the basin from Huyana then left them to it, her own breasts aching as she heard the baby begin to suckle and Catherine's cooing as she was engulfed by maternal love.

* * * *

Finally, as darkness fell, Rosie heard the thundering of horses' hooves. That had to be the men.

She opened the front door and peered into the night. Sure enough, three horses approached the perimeter fence. Two of the men jumped down from their mounts and hurried toward the house while the third one, Rosie suspected it was Emmett, took the mares over to the barn.

Kenan reached her first.

"Is she…is it…I've been so…" He leaned over his knees and gasped for breath.

"Just get inside, you fool. Catherine is well. She's waiting for you."

He obeyed and Rosie turned back to the porch.

There *he* was. Dusty. Tired. Road weary. But as handsome as she remembered.

"Joshua." She whispered his name then sighed as he took her into his arms. She relaxed against him, allowing his strength and vitality to form their reassuring circle around her.

"Oh, Rosie, I've missed you so much. Has the baby arrived? Are you all right? Each time I'm away, it gets harder, I swear."

You have no idea…

"Yes, Catherine is very well. She and Kenan have a daughter. And how are you?" She pulled out of his embrace and looked at him. Even in the semi-darkness, with his face illuminated only by the light from within the house, his eyes seemed intense as the sky on a clear summer's day. They burned into her, reaching down inside her and igniting her passion for him. But this would not do. She had to end this. She had to divorce herself from her feelings for him so that she could bid him farewell.

She did. It was true.

But an idea began to form. She *would* tell Joshua that they had no future, that he should leave and never return. But she could allow herself something before she severed their ties. *Why not?* If she was to experience a lifetime of suffering, an eternity of heartbreak in a cold, lonely bed, then she could give herself something first...some sweet memories to treasure for the rest of her days.

After all, she might never have the opportunity to be with a man again. She shivered. She would not want to be with another man. Joshua was the only man she had ever wanted, ever loved. So, before she sent him off to live his life at the Hampton ranch, she would give herself to him. She would be with him as his wife, in body, mind and heart, if not as his legal bride.

Mr. Hampton couldn't take that away from her, and it gave her some comfort. An act of rebellion, mayhap, but one that she wanted. She had longed to lie with Joshua over the months of their courtship and they had nearly succumbed on several occasions, but the insecurity of being unable to confirm exactly when they might marry had kept them chaste. Joshua had feared getting her with child or taking her honor and not being able to make an honest woman of her as quickly as he would've liked. So they had waited. And it had been difficult. Virtue wasn't always an easy option.

But there was no sense in delaying any longer. Tomorrow would not come. She would take what she could today.

"Yes, Rosie, I am well now that I'm here with you."

He squeezed her against his chest and her stomach flipped. His hard male body made her own seem soft and pliant, and her breasts tingled deliciously. She felt the familiar stirring between her legs that she always did whenever Joshua held her close. It made her long to strip away her clothing so she could feel him, skin to skin, the curves of her own body fitted against the solid planes of his.

Joshua tilted her chin and lowered his lips to hers. He smelled of fresh air, horses, leather and hay. *Divine.*

Rosie kissed him back, opening her mouth to take his tongue. She moaned as he plundered her, his kisses growing more ardent by the second. She squirmed when she felt the intriguing hardening at his groin, the impressive length of his masculinity that she yearned to see and caress with her hands, her mouth, her hidden flesh.

And why not? She wanted Joshua. He clearly wanted her. She had been good for so long. *Too long.*

She tore herself away from his kiss. "Can I get you a drink? Some food?"

He shook his head. "No, Rosie." His gaze was unflinching, penetrating, full of desire. "The only thing I want...the only thing I need right now is time with you."

Rosie glanced behind her into the house. Kenan must have gone in to see Catherine. They would, no doubt, be gazing at their beautiful daughter for hours to come. She could hear Matthew and Huyana talking at the kitchen table, and occasionally, she heard the young woman laugh softly. Her kindly younger brother was already absorbed by the honey-skinned woman. It pleased her to think that he had found someone he liked, someone he might even now be envisaging a future with.

So they were all busy. Except for Emmett. And he was in the barn. The quiet, private place where she would like to spend time with Joshua.

As if he'd heard her thoughts, Emmett suddenly appeared. "Hey, Rosie, what happened? Is Catherine safe?"

"Yes, Emmett. She was delivered of a girl. Both mother and child are well."

Emmett grinned. "So we have a niece. That's great to hear. Now I'm starving. What's for supper?"

Rosie laughed. Emmett was a good-natured young man, but typical in his need to be fed and watered as soon as he arrived home. "There's chicken stew in the pot."

"Wonderful. You two eating?" Emmett flicked his gaze over them both in turn and raised his eyebrows. "I guess not. See you later." With that, he bounded into the house, and Rosie heard Matthew's growl of disapproval as Emmett attacked him in his usual *look out I'm home, brother* way. Emmett would have no idea what thoughts now ran amok in Rosie's mind. He would think merely that his innocent older sister wanted to speak with Joshua, that she longed to hear the rancher's stories of the trail and about how much he had missed her. He would harbor no suspicions that sensible, careful Rosie was considering throwing caution—and her virtue—to the wind.

Why would he, when Rosie was even surprising herself?

As Joshua closed the barn door behind them, Rosie shivered. The evening was cool, it was true, but she was also nervous. And excited. And devastated at the thought of having to give Joshua up.

Not now. Don't think on it now. Be with him as you've wanted to...deal with losing him in the cold light of day.

She watched as Joshua lit a kerosene lamp and hung it on a peg.

"Rosie." Joshua reached out and took her hands. He pulled her closer to him, so that her head rested on his strong chest. She could hear the steady beat of his heart, his life force, the core of his strength and love.

In this moment, it was hers. All that mattered was right here and now. He rocked her gently in his arms as if dancing to music that only he could hear. The straw rustled beneath their feet and sent up the fresh, earthy scent of summer fields and endless carefree days spent under the hot, blue Montana skies.

Joshua ran his hands over her back and she relaxed against him. His touch was so good, so strong, so right. He stroked her hair then released it from its bun, tracing its waves as they tumbled down to her waist. It made little ripples of delight shoot up her back and over her scalp. She snaked her own hands up around his neck then lifted her head for his kiss.

"Joshua…"

"Rosie."

"I want—"She stole a steadying breath. "I want more tonight."

He leaned backward to look at her.

"More?"

"I want to be with you properly."

"Rosie…what…I mean…but we agreed that we would wait."

"I'm tired of waiting." She bit her lip at her boldness. To push for something she wanted was out of character. She usually went along with others, did what she could to please her brothers and Catherine. She was accepting, placid, calm—the voice of reason and compassion. But now she was being forced to surrender the love she had waited her whole life for and it made her bold, brave, fierce. At least regarding how she bid it goodbye. "Joshua, I want you to make love to me."

"Rosie, I don't know. I…*we*…have waited this long. Don't you think we should hold on a bit longer?"

Rosie grinned at the dark hue that stole up his neck and spread across his cheeks. This was difficult for him. He was a man. He had needs. But he had shown her respect and not acted—not fully anyway—upon those needs. Now she was offering herself to him. Everything that she had to give.

"I really mean it, Joshua. We've waited long enough. The time is right. It's now or never." Her throat constricted at the final word. Joshua had no idea how literal her words were.

"Are you sure?"

Rosie recognized hope in his eyes. He was a good man, a loyal man, but he had been torn. He was still young, yet he made her feel protected, safe, adored. He was all male. His strength and confidence enveloped Rosie whenever she was with him, and she had believed that her life with him would be a happy one. She swallowed hard at the surge of pain in her throat.

"Yes, Joshua. More certain than I have ever been about anything."

He paused for a moment and Rosie knew that he was thinking it through, weighing it up. He would never act without thinking, this handsome man of hers.

No, not mine, not anymore.

"I'll be gentle, I swear. I'll take it slow. If you want me to stop at any point, my darling, you just say. I only want what you want, Rosie. My wife-to-be."

She looked away at that, the sincerity in his gaze too much to bear.

His wife? Oh, Joshua, if only you knew. This cannot be. This is goodbye.

He scooped her into his arms and carried her away from her distressing thoughts and into one of the empty stalls. She could hear the quiet breathing of the animals nearby, the horses snorting and the piglets suckling at their mother's dugs. The earthy scent of the animals and the straw was all around them, comforting, familiar and primitive. Her heart thundered and her stomach tightened as Joshua laid her down on a bed of hay. It was soft beneath her, fresh and clean, reminding her of happy sunny days on the plains.

When Joshua stroked her all over, from the top of her head to the tips of her toes, she closed her eyes to savor his touch — to remember this moment in all of its sensual glory. Then he began to undress her, very slowly, cautiously and respectfully, and Rosie held her breath, afraid to exhale in case she disturbed his ardent concentration.

Joshua tried to slow his breathing, but he was so churned up, he felt he'd explode any second. How had he ended up here, like this, undressing Rosie?

Sure, they'd been alone before. It was accepted by her family that they'd soon marry and Kenan trusted him. He knew that. So he shouldn't betray that trust, should he? Joshua felt that he'd done well so far, behaved like a gentleman. Although he had kissed and caressed Rosie, he'd done no more. Most nights, he left the barn with a cock as hard as stone and a brow as hot as the plains in summer, but Rosie was worth it. She deserved respect. He loved the woman and he wanted to give her everything.

She lay before him now, sweet, innocent and beautiful. She might be his elder by seven years but it didn't matter at all to him. Why would it? His folks had muttered about it a few times but he just saw Rosie. Not her age. Not their difference in years. Just a kind, caring, compassionate woman in need of a good man to take her to wife.

And that was what Joshua wanted to do.

So why had it taken him so long? The sense of shame washed over him again. He had been such a clumsy fool around Rosie at first. She was so beautiful, graceful and wise. He'd been afraid to speak in front of her for weeks in case he said something that made her believe he was stupid. But her kindness and her cool, calm demeanor had soon helped him to relax, and before he knew it, he was as comfortable with her as with her twin brother.

He had wanted to propose for a while, but something was still holding him back. He'd been saving his wages to build them a house and nearly had enough, but it wasn't that. He knew what it was. And it made him cold to his boots.

He was afraid of how his folks would react. He'd witnessed their disapproval when Kenan and Catherine got wed, but had tried to convince himself that if he gave it some time before speaking to them about Rosie, then their doubts would fade and they would approve of his choice of bride. But recent comments from them suggested that they hadn't changed their minds. As far as they were concerned, Catherine was a harlot, tainted by her Indian abduction...if that was what had even happened. So, by association, Rosie was tainted, too. He felt the familiar twitching of the small muscle in his jaw that told of his anxiety. Add to the boiling pot Rosie's age, and Dylan Hampton and his wife were not at all overjoyed at where Joshua's affections lay.

It was made even more difficult by his father's decline in health over the last year. Dylan Hampton had always been a proud and independent man, and the loss of his strength and vitality had hit him hard. Joshua knew that his pa was having a hard time accepting that he was no longer as strong and energetic as he'd once been. That was a part of aging though, surely. But Joshua also knew, as much as he hated to admit it, that there was more to it than just getting older. Dylan Hampton was ill. Something was eating him up from the inside and at times it seemed that it was only the older man's stubbornness that stopped him from giving in altogether. But his pa's illness made him worry about making him mad. Renowned for rages that made his family tremble and head for the hills whenever they sensed one brewing, Dylan Hampton could well cause himself injury if his temper got the better of him. Joshua just didn't want to be responsible for causing his pa more pain. And asking for his pa's blessing to wed Rosie might just be the kindling that set Dylan Hampton ablaze.

He shook his head to clear the negativity. Here he was, dwelling on the darker things in his life when he had the brightest one in front of him, flushed with desire. He could make love to Rosie here and now. Finally. Seal their love. There would certainly be no going back then. He would never let his father sway his decision once he'd lain with Rosie. That would be reprehensible. It gave him strength and confirmed to him what he already knew deep in his heart—Rosie mattered more to him than anyone, or anything, ever had or ever would.

He finished unbuttoning Rosie's housedress and gently pushed the material apart. His heart thundered at what he saw. His cock hardened and his mouth dried up. A thin cotton chemise covered her breasts and her dark nipples showed through the material.

"Oh, Rosie."

"Joshua. What's wrong?"

"Nothing is wrong, sweetheart. It's just...you're so beautiful. I want you so much."

"I want you too, my love."

She sat up and he smiled at the hay caught in her hair. Her eyes shone, her lips were red and slightly parted. She didn't appear innocent right now with her dress gaping and her come-to-bed gaze.

She shrugged her arms out of her dress and pushed it to her waist then knelt and took his hands in hers. "Do you want to continue?"

"Yes."

"Then do."

She placed his fingers on the lacing of her corset and helped him to undo the bow.

His fingers shook as he loosened the laces until he could free her from the restrictive undergarment. She lifted her arms and he slipped it over her head. If she was nervous then she wasn't letting it show. Her sudden confidence aroused him further because it convinced him that she wanted him, that it was acceptable to do this here and now.

Joshua dropped the corset on the hay then returned his gaze to her. Through the white cotton, he could make out the perfect orbs of her breasts. He had fondled them before, shyly, over her clothing, but never seen them naked. Now he would.

He reached trembling hands toward the woman he loved but stopped before he actually touched her.

"This is what I want, Joshua."

"It is?"

Rosie leaned forward so that her breasts pushed into his hands. Full. Round. Warm. Soft.

"Stand up. I need to get this dress off you." His voice was husky, so low that it was barely audible.

She did as he commanded and he tugged the dress down. She stood before him in just her chemise and stockings. He helped her out of her boots then rested his hands on the hot, smooth skin of her thighs. As if reading his thoughts, Rosie slid down to her knees, which meant that his hands pushed the flimsy material of her chemise up. He gasped as her upper thighs were revealed to him. No bloomers. The blood rushed through his head and he took deep gulps of air for a moment to steady himself.

When the spots had stopped dancing before his eyes, he eased Rosie onto her back again and nudged her legs apart. At the edge of the white undergarment, he could make out the shadow of dark hair that covered her sex. It took all of his strength not to whip out his cock and thrust into her instantly. But he wouldn't do that to her. This was Rosie. The woman he adored. The woman he wanted to love and protect all his days. The fact that she had such an effect on him could only be a good thing. Not only did he love her, but he desired her too. He would be gentle, tender, take things slowly.

Savor this precious moment. Their first time.

Rosie pressed her nails into her palms. Her stomach was tight and she quivered from head to toe. She could stop this now, could tell Joshua that she wasn't ready, that she wanted to wait. But she wouldn't do that. She wanted him. Even through her nerves, she sizzled with raw, unfettered longing for this man.

Now.

Before she had to turn him away forever.

He unbuttoned his shirt and pulled it over his head then stepped out of his trousers and boots. His union suit bulged at his groin and it made Rosie tremble to see the evidence of his desire. His broad shoulders and strong, muscular forearms quickened her heartbeat and sent heat rushing to her forbidden parts.

As Joshua removed his union suit and stood before her naked, Rosie knew what it was to be stunned into silence. He was perfect. From his sandy hair to his strong calves with their golden fuzz, he was pure man. His chest was defined and smooth. His stomach rippled with tight muscles, which made him seem like he'd been carved out of wood by a master carpenter. And his cock... She almost giggled at the word she'd heard her brothers use, but it seemed so appropriate now that she could see it.

It protruded from his body. Long. Thick. Dusky pink. Purple veined. Rosie clenched her hands over her stomach as she realized what Joshua was about to do. How could she take him...take his large member inside her?

Joshua lowered himself to rest on his elbows above her.

"Are you all right, Rosie?"

She reached out and caressed his cheek, gazing into his blue eyes.

"Yes, Joshua. A little nervous, but I want this. I need to be with you."

"Oh my angel," he whispered as he slid her shift above her hips and brushed the back of his hand over her mound.

Rosie tensed, waiting to feel him pushing his cock between her legs. But he didn't. Instead, he continued caressing her until she moaned with need. He slipped his fingers between her folds and touched her everywhere, from her hard bud to the tight entrance of her body. At first, it was strange, even tickly, but as he continued, every touch made her desire grow. He moved his thumb in a circular motion until she began to move with him, lifting her hips to meet him. So when he finally pushed a finger inside her, she took him easily and gratefully, moaning as he probed her gently before adding another.

"Do you like that, Rosie?"

"Yes…so much."

"How about this?"

He moved down her body, kissing her breasts through her chemise and nibbling at her hard nipples. Then he kissed her belly and blew into her navel, tracing its hollow with his tongue. When he moved lower still, she gasped. He couldn't do that. He shouldn't. Surely?

"Relax, sweetheart. This should feel good."

Rosie sank into the hay as Joshua covered her sex with his lips and tongue. He sucked and licked until she could control herself no longer and she bucked against him, begging him for more and more and more. When she reached a sudden point of no return, heat surged through her body, starting at her core then flooding through her limbs. She writhed beneath him, wanting it to last forever, mewling as each spasm left a reminder of the intensity she had experienced just seconds before.

As the delicious sensations ebbed away and Joshua crawled back up her body, Rosie's cheeks glowed.

"What just happened?" she croaked, her throat restricted by emotion.

"I pleasured you, my love. Did you like it?" He grinned, and Rosie realized that he was proud.

"It was wonderful, Joshua."

"I've never done that before," he admitted, blushing.

"I'm glad to hear that, but you were very skilled."

"Thank you, Rosie. It was a pleasure."

"It was indeed."

"Anytime, ma'am." He winked wickedly.

Rosie swallowed hard to dislodge the lump that swelled in her throat. *Anytime?* How she wished it could be true. But Joshua's sweet, hot kisses would belong to another. She had but a temporary hold on them. On him.

"Do you feel...ready now? To try..." He nudged her with his erection, dragging her from sadness to the sweet sharpness of arousal. He pushed the head of his cock between her wet folds and she opened her legs wider in response.

"I think so. I believe that I am."

"I'll take it slowly."

"Joshua?" She didn't want to ask but she had to know.

"Yes?"

"Have you..." She blinked, ashamed. She had no right to ask him. And she might not like the answer.

"No, Rosie. I have never done this before. Unusual, I know, for a man of my age, but though I've...done some things along the way, I've never made love to a woman. You're my first, too. I've been waiting for you." The color in his cheeks heightened and Rosie felt as if she would burst. Joshua had never lain with a woman before and she would be his first. It was as if this was meant to be all along. Her heart swelled with love and her core pulsed as he eased his way inside.

There was an initial resistance but Joshua pumped his hips against her, spreading her lubrication to ease himself deeper. Rosie gasped at the momentary flicker of pain when he gained full entry but it was over as soon as it had begun. Then Joshua lifted himself onto his elbows and thrust, again and again and again. He increased the speed of his movements and Rosie wrapped her legs around his waist and gave herself to him, savoring his thick, hard length as he drove it deeper. The friction made her bud swell again and she ground against him, needing his closeness, his cock, his touch. She was full of him and he became part of her, an extension of her heart.

Joshua suddenly froze and kissed her hard before pulsing into her with one final, impassioned thrust. He swelled in her depths then twitched and his heat filled her body. The culmination of his desire overwhelmed her and she shuddered too, consumed again by intense, satisfying pleasure and the overwhelming rush of love.

"Why have we waited so long to do this?" She whispered the question into his thick hair as he laid his head on her chest.

"I was holding out, Rosie. Trying to be a gentleman. Trying to do right by you."

"You have always done right by me, Joshua."

He raised his head to look at her. "No, Rosie, I should have pr—"

She placed a finger over his lips to silence his protest. "You are a good man, Joshua. Never forget that."

"I love you, sweetheart."

She pressed his head back onto her breast, watching as it rose and fell with the rapid beating of her heart, and willed herself not to break down. He was a good man. He had been thinking of her virtue. Perhaps also protecting their hearts. Because now that they'd been as close as a man and woman could be, Rosie had no idea how she would be able to walk away from Joshua. The man she adored. The man she longed to call husband. The man she yearned to have a future with.

A future that wasn't hers to have.

Chapter Four

"What is it, Rosie?" Catherine strolled onto the porch, her sleeping baby peaceful in her arms. Rosie was amazed at how quickly little Rebecca was growing. It had taken Catherine and Kenan a while to name her, but the name they had chosen was just perfect. Rebecca seemed to change by the day and she had rapidly outgrown the tiny outfits that she and Catherine had embroidered for her early weeks.

Rosie admired Catherine's beauty. She was the picture of contentment. Her face was full and round, her cheeks were flushed with happiness and her eyes shone with joy.

Rosie released the porch handrail and smiled at her sister-in-law. "I'm fine, Catherine. Just a bit tired is all."

"Nearly three months of this little one squawking through the night, perhaps?" Catherine smiled.

"No. I'm fine with that. I never did sleep deeply. Besides, I love to hear her in the night. It's like she wants us all to know she's around."

"She certainly does." Catherine grinned. "But something's wrong with you, Rosie, I can tell. What is it? You seem...lost... As if you're not fully present."

"I really am tired, Catherine. And I feel...a bit queasy, I guess. Though I don't think that the chicken stew we ate last night was bad."

"There was nothing wrong with the stew, Rosie. Nothing at all. Don't try to distract me. Have you a female ailment...one you need to see a doctor about?"

Rosie waved her hand, dismissing her sister-in-law's concerns. "I've been doing a lot of thinking of late..."

Catherine frowned. "About what?"

"Well, you know that Joshua and I have been...we are...well, I..."

"You love him, Rosie, and he loves you. It's as clear as a mountain spring. Has he proposed yet? I guess that you'd tell us straightaway if he did...unless for some reason you were holding out. But I can't for the life of me think why you might when it would be such good news and all..."

Rosie winced at the directness of the question and Catherine's jumbled words. He hadn't proposed marriage. But that was a good thing, right? It would make everything easier when it came to saying goodbye. So why did it hurt so much? Rosie knew that she had to make the break and make it soon. She couldn't continue here, playing at being his wife in everything but name, looking forward to seeing him each and every day and living for the times when they were alone. She just couldn't. But although her resolve had been strong on that day when Mr. Hampton had visited, it had seeped away slowly. Holding Joshua, kissing him and being held against his strong chest had all weakened her until she had been content to tell herself that she'd do it tomorrow. Or the next day.

Knowing, deep down, that it would be no easier then, yet trying to convince herself that it would be. So three months had passed and she had yet to tell him to forget about her, to return to his father's ranch and leave her in peace. Though what kind of peace it would be, she had no idea. How could she find peace without the man she craved, loved, adored?

As the time had passed, Rosie had dreaded hearing Joshua ask for her hand in marriage, yet longed for it. Rosie found herself softening. Perhaps it was being around new mother Catherine and the beautiful little babe but. If Joshua proposed, then maybe they could find a way around the situation. Maybe. It was doubtful. How could they? What would change? But...just maybe. Kenan and Catherine had found a way...

However, Joshua had not asked, so she had allowed herself that little bit longer to enjoy being with him.

Little bit longer? Try three whole months. As his lover.

She was shocked at her own wanton behavior. Yet not shocked. She couldn't quite fathom how this worked, but it was as if she were looking at it from a distance. From someone else's perspective. It could've been grief at the prospect of being torn from Joshua's arms. It could be the lack of sleep. She was frequently woken throughout the night by the baby's hungry demands or her need to be soothed and rocked until she dozed off again. Rosie often took over for Catherine when exhaustion claimed her sister-in-law, and she was happy to walk the length of the homestead with the warm little body pressed to her chest as she crooned old Irish lullabies and whispered of the future little Rebecca could have. Or it could just be that she really, really did not want to lose him.

But it was time to end things. She could not and would not continue in this manner. The constant fear of when she would be forced to send Joshua away was clearly taking its toll on her body and her mind, and it would soon begin to affect those around her. She could not allow that to happen to her precious family.

The baby whimpered. Catherine shifted her up onto her shoulder and patted her back. Rosie's heart leaped to see the easy confidence that her sister-in-law displayed. It must be wonderful to have a child. Incredible. She ran a hand over her own belly, sadness washing over her as she imagined how empty it was. And always would be.

Nausea swelled in her throat and she leaned forward, gulping in air.

"Rosie? Whatever is wrong?" Catherine approached her and stood so close that Rosie felt the younger woman's warmth through her skirts. "I take it that he hasn't asked you then?"

Rosie shook her head.

"I cannot understand it." Catherine paused. "Oh Rosie...is it because of me?" She took a step back. Rosie turned and looked at her and winced at the ashen shade of Catherine's face. "Oh no, dear heart. Dear, dear Rosie. Has Joshua decided that he cannot wed you because of your link to me?"

Rosie watched as Catherine's big green eyes filled with tears. She held the baby tightly against her shoulder and rocked from side to side, causing her gray skirts to swing around her legs.

"No, Catherine. No, it's not because of you. Why would you think that?" Rosie couldn't allow Catherine to blame herself, even though Mr. Hampton had named Catherine as one reason for his disapproval of a union between Rosie and his son.

Catherine had been through so much, and now she had found happiness. Rosie would not see that destroyed. "This has nothing to do with your past, Catherine. *Nothing*. It is more because of me." Heat filled her cheeks and she glanced away for a moment at the green plains beyond the perimeter fence, drawing strength from the beautiful landscape she had grown up loving. "It is because of…my age."

"Your age?" Catherine moved closer to Rosie and freed a hand from her child. She placed it on Rosie's arm and rubbed gently. The gesture made Rosie's throat ache.

"I'm nearly thirty-three, Catherine. Hardly young and fruitful. What if I can't bear a child?"

"Rosie, women older than you have children. You're so young in your appearance and fit and healthy. You'll have no problems, I'm sure of it."

"Yes. Maybe. But perhaps it's a chance that Joshua shouldn't take."

"You really love him."

"Yes." Rosie bit the inside of her cheeks hard. She must not start crying. If she did, she feared that she would never stop. Determination filled her. Fuelled her. She couldn't stay around and wait for Joshua to alienate his family. He would, she knew that, if she asked it of him. He was a kind and decent man and he would do right by her. But it would tear him apart if his family disowned him. And there was Catherine. The sweet girl would blame herself if Rosie refused Joshua's proposal then stayed around at the homestead to wallow in her heartbreak. Catherine would believe that she was to blame. Rosie couldn't see that happen. "But sometimes when we love someone, we have to let them go."

"So what will you do? I cannot imagine how you...or Joshua...can be happy without each other. You seem so close and so happy, so right for each other."

"I have a desire to travel a little," Rosie lied, lifting her chin to prevent the fall of tears that Catherine's words had conjured. "To see some of America. I've been thinking on it a while."

Catherine's mouth fell open. "Does Kenan know?"

"Not yet." Rosie thought of her twin brother's reaction. He would not allow it. An unmarried woman traveling alone, unchaperoned. Kenan would be furious and likely blame Joshua. She couldn't allow that either. "Please don't tell him, Catherine. I'll speak to him about it. Soon."

Catherine nodded. The baby wriggled in her arms, smacking her tiny lips together. "This little one needs feeding. But we will talk more about this."

"Yes, of course." Rosie watched Catherine walk inside then she stepped off the porch and crossed the yard toward the chicken coop. The hens fluttered greedily around her ankles, hoping that she'd come to feed them. *The hens I reared.*

She looked around at the homestead she'd kept in order — from the small vegetable patch to the pigsty — never dreaming that she would ever leave. Unless it was to be wed. But now she would leave for another reason. To free the people she loved from their duty to her. She loved them all. She would not be their reason for heartache. She would leave before that became a reality. She would leave before her own pain prevented her from doing what she had intended doing three months ago, before she allowed herself to become one with Joshua, before she had completely surrendered to her own heart.

Chapter Five

Joshua leaned against the fence of the horse pen and watched as his eighteen-year-old brother, Clarence, rode around on their newest acquisition, a gray stallion that Dylan Hampton had invested in for breeding. The cattle side of the business was doing well and now their ambitious father planned to develop in the equine arena, too. He had even suggested that Joshua might want to manage this area of the business once it was up and running.

The ranch was a busy place. As well as the Hampton family members — spanning three generations — it swarmed with ranch hands, some of their wives and children, and a variety of beasts. Dylan Hampton was a good employer and had a respected name, so he tended to retain his workers for longer than many other ranch owners. Workers were content to hang around for months, even years, and their loyalty meant that they worked hard and didn't shirk like many of the traveling ranch hands.

In fact, no one at the ranch shirked. Joshua's siblings had no sense of entitlement as might be expected from folks who had grown up with food in their bellies and clean clothes on their backs.

That was what made this whole situation with Rosie so difficult. He wanted to do things the right way. His father was so self-assured, so determined. He'd built his business up from scratch and was a proud man. A good husband and father. But he also ruled his roost without sentimentality. Women were for childbearing and homemaking, not for silly notions about romance and love. Joshua's own mother, while providing hot meals and clean clothes, did not coddle her children into being soft and overly affectionate. Joshua knew that he was loved but he also knew that he had to play his part. He couldn't let his family down. Couldn't upset his father while he was unwell.

Yet he couldn't neglect his loyalty to Rosie either. And Joshua had to accept that his father might not get any better.

The time had come to face up to his responsibilities. *All of them.* He had tried to broach the subject with his father before, but always seemed to digress, and he hated himself for it. He was not the eldest son, so all of the weight did not fall on his shoulders and he was glad of that. Dylan Junior carried that burden. In fact, Joshua was the fourth child of ten. Yet he had never felt that he was less important than the others, or more important. Dylan Hampton was always fair.

But it meant that he was unable to do anything that might bring the family name into disrepute. Just last year his brother Billy, three years his junior, had gotten Rita Mae Hudson with child. They had married quickly, Dylan Hampton refusing to allow the scandal of a bastard child to grace his threshold. Yet Billy and Rita had acted as carefree as wild horses racing across the plains. They'd laughed and danced at their wedding and had taken to parenthood immediately, rejoicing in the challenges of rearing a young family.

Why was it so easy for Billy? Joshua wished that he could be that lighthearted about things, that he didn't give a damn about his folks' opinions of him. But he just couldn't do it. It tore him apart to think of how he would have to disappoint them. But he would. Because he wanted Rosie. It was now or never and he wasn't about to risk losing her. And he couldn't accept that Rosie was a disappointment for anyone anyway. How could she be when she was so lovely?

"So what's eating you, son?"

Joshua turned to face his father. Dylan Hampton leaned against the fence, his large frame causing the wooden posts to creak. Joshua was almost the same height as his father, yet he felt the other man's will extend and attempt to dominate him. As it always had. It made his father seem bigger, broader, younger.

"I need to tell you something. I should have told you weeks...months ago, Pa, but it just never seemed like the right time."

"Joshua..." Dylan Hampton reached out a big hand and squeezed his shoulder. The action was at once reassuring and daunting—it was as if his father was reminding him of his place at the ranch. "Some things are better left unsaid."

"I'm not sure if that's true, Pa." Joshua's stomach lurched and his heart upped its pace. Why did he feel like a child whenever his father took that tone?

"Listen, son. Whatever's on your mind, it won't bother you in a month or two. Maybe less than that. You're a young man. You've a whole life ahead of you. You'll soon forget and your heart will mend."

"How do you know? In fact, *what* do you know about it?" Joshua felt the rage of distress building. Did his father know that he wanted to speak to him about Rosie? It sounded like he did and that he was convinced that Joshua was mistaken about his feelings, that he still viewed him as a child to be steered in the right direction.

"Son, it's natural for a young man of your age to feel attracted to a handsome woman. Hell knows, I've been there myself a few times. But it's better to get it out of your system then move on. Go into town, visit a cathouse. Take a few days. Whatever you need. But don't go thinking on marrying some wench just because she's sweet and kind and because she makes you hard."

"What?" Rage boiled in the pit of Joshua's stomach and a red mist clouded his vision. The sounds of the ranch seemed far away and he gazed across the training pen, unable to focus on anything.

"I'll not watch you throw your life away on an aging woman just because you've got some romantic notion in your head. You need to find yourself a young filly, fit to breed. Carrying a child is hard on a woman and the younger she is the better. A woman past thirty" — he shook his head — "is taking a big risk, son, especially with a first birth. Even if she delivers a babe safely, there's no guarantees that there won't be something wrong with it. And if she doesn't…"

Joshua struggled to breathe. He felt as if his lungs were being squashed. How could his father be so prejudiced, so narrow-minded? When Joshua thought of Rosie, it wasn't of a woman to make love to then abandon. It wasn't of a woman to breed from. He saw Rosie as so many wonderful things. She was sweet and kind and beautiful. She was, now that he could be completely honest about it, *everything* to him. He wanted a wife, a partner, a lover and a friend.

"Now, Pa. You've no right speaking about Rosie Duggan like that."

Dylan Hampton scowled, his thick eyebrows like storm clouds over his milky blue eyes, and Joshua recognized the look that had made him quake as a child. Once Dylan Hampton's raging disappointment settled on the horizon, there was no telling when it might lift. It blocked out the sun, the moon, the stars and all hope of any joy. When it lifted, the whole family breathed a collective sigh of relief and did their utmost to ensure that it didn't return again anytime soon. Joshua knew that his brothers would not thank him for his obstinacy even though most of them were grown men now.

"So you admit that it's the Duggan mare."

Joshua forced air into his lungs. "She's no horse, Pa. No filly, no mare. She's a warm-blooded woman with a mind of her own. She has thoughts and feelings and a loving heart. She is tender and considerate. Intelligent and —

Dylan Hampton smacked his broad forehead with his hand then rubbed it down over his cheeks. The palm rasped against his salt and pepper stubble. "So you are in love with her?"

Joshua nodded. "And I want to take her to wife."

"A foolish notion, son."

Joshua watched a tiny muscle in his father's cheek twitch.

"To you it seems that way, but for me it's different, Pa. I need to be with her. She's the sweetest woman I've ever met."

"Sweet won't bear you strong sons, Joshua."

"I don't care."

"*Now* you don't...but what about in five or ten years' time? You're still young. Too young to know how important it is to have a legacy. To leave something behind. This life is so damned short, Joshua." Dylan paused and Joshua noticed the Adam's apple bobbing furiously in his father's throat. "Shorter for some...than others. You'll want children, I don't doubt it. A man needs to feel that he'll go on somehow. That his passing won't be the end of him. Pah! Who knows if there really is a life after this one. I struggle to accept that there could be though I long to believe that there is." Dylan's voice broke on the final word.

Joshua stared hard at his father's profile. What was wrong with him? He seemed so emotional. Pensive. Afraid. And Joshua had never, ever seen fear pass over his father's features before. His ailment was affecting him more than he was letting on.

"Pa, I understand what you're saying. At least I think I do." *And I don't want to hurt you or disappoint you.*

"One day you'll understand, son. Just not for a while. Least I hope not, anyhow." Dylan laid a heavy hand on Joshua's shoulder.

"I just want you to understand that I love Rosie. I can't bear the thought of my life without her."

"And what if you do get her with child? What if she dies giving birth?"

Pain filled Joshua's chest and he rubbed absently at his shirt front. Losing Rosie as she gave birth to his child? It was an image that threatened to rip him apart. Was his father right?

"I...that won't happen."

"Guarantee it, can you?"

"It could happen to anyone, Pa."

"True" — Dylan nodded — "but it's more likely when a woman is older."

Joshua gazed at his father. Were his motives only centered on his concerns or was there more to it? Joshua had been so certain just moments ago that he should go ahead and follow his heart—that he should take Rosie to wife and be damned with it all. He loved her. She loved him. But now, doubt settled all around him, the way it always did whenever Dylan Hampton wanted his own way about something. It was a strong will that had built a ranch from scratch to create a thriving business, and a strong will that kept it improving year after year.

Was love enough? Could Joshua really offer Rosie happiness and all that she deserved, or was he being selfish because he wanted her?

"All I'm saying, son, is that you need to think long and hard about it. Marriage is a lifelong commitment. It don't mean that a man can't have some fun elsewhere from time to time, but it sure does mean that you owe your wife a home and food on the table. All this"—he gestured around at the ranch—"it'll be yours and your brothers' when I go. You've a lot to offer a woman in terms of stability. But placing a woman in danger by getting her with child when she's past her youth, well that ain't fair on her. I'm sure you don't want that for Rosie Duggan if you care about her as much as you say you do."

"I..." Joshua opened and closed his mouth, trying in vain to find the words to articulate exactly how he felt.

"And, Joshua, there's the other distasteful matter."

"What?" Joshua met his father's eyes. All he could see was raw honesty staring back at him. Dylan Hampton had no reason to lie. No reason at all. He knew what he believed and that was all he would see. His stubborn Irish roots kept him planted and they were too strong to tear up.

"That wife of Kenan Duggan."

"What about her?" Joshua knew what his father referred to but he wanted to hear him say it.

"Her, uh, abduction. It's still a mystery exactly what happened there."

"It's nobody's business, that's why."

"Maybe not, but if a son of mine is thinking on marrying into that family then I see it as my business. You think I can risk being associated with a family tainted with an Indian whore?"

"Now hold on a minute..." Joshua's shoulders burned with tension and he closed his hands into fists at his sides, digging the short nails into his palms. "How can you just assume that she was taken by the Sioux?" He wanted to remain calm. He had just witnessed his father's vulnerability, and the last thing he wanted was to explode on the older man. But Dylan was making it so darned hard for him.

"That's the story her aunt and uncle spread around when she disappeared. We might not know if it's true but it's the version that's out there." Dylan Hampton shrugged. "You think I want to go around saying to folks that my son married into the Duggans, who keep a harlot at their homestead...and an Indian harlot to boot!"

Joshua ground his teeth together. He hated to admit it but his father was right on this one. It would be bad for their family reputation and Dylan Hampton had literally bled, sweated and toiled to build his business. Folks were distrustful and times were hard, so the last thing the Hamptons needed was a scandal—even by association. But it was so unfair. So prejudiced. Kenan and Catherine loved each other. It was no one's business what had happened to her in the two years when she'd been away. Kenan loved her regardless and it shouldn't matter to anyone else. But it did. That much was evident.

"So what do I do, Pa?"

"I think you know the answer to that one now, Joshua, don't you? Do the right thing for Rosie Duggan, for yourself and for our family. I know you'll do the decent thing. You're a good man."

Dylan slapped Joshua on the shoulder then turned and loped away. His large frame was hunched over, as if trying to protect his core from invisible punches. He only straightened up when he reached the barn where the stable buck was painting tar onto a mule's hoof.

Big decisions loomed, their weight strapped to Joshua's back, squeezing his ribs tight over his lungs so that he had to take deep gulps of air to fill them.

The ranch would continue to thrive whether Joshua was here or not. He had grown up riding horses, following the cattle trail and working every day to earn his keep. As a young man, he had striven to prove to his father that he was worthy of respect. He had longed to be able to show that he was just as good as his brothers. Perhaps it was some sort of sibling rivalry, a competitive edge that drove him on, kept him wanting to bask in the glow of his father's approval. But lately, although he certainly didn't want to anger his pa, he just hadn't been as concerned about earning Dylan Hampton's praise as when he was younger.

Meeting Rosie last year had turned his beliefs about what he wanted in life upside down. He'd never been with a woman before, never known a woman that intimately. It had churned him up and left him all confused. He wanted to offer Rosie all that she could desire. Dylan Hampton's words hadn't changed that.

He would worry about Rosie if they got married and she became pregnant, it was true. But if he didn't marry her, then he would worry about her even more. Either way, someone would be hurt or upset. Was this about finding his way as a man? Was this what happened to a man when he fell in love? His family still mattered, but the object of his affection mattered more. Surely it was nature's way.

So why procrastinate any longer?

Hurting his own family by soiling their good name was the last thing he wanted to do. Out of the ten Hampton children, he felt sure that he was the one who seemed to worry the most about upsetting their father. He hated being so damned sensitive at times and longed for the devil-may-care attitude of Billy or the self-assured arrogance of Dylan Junior. But he couldn't change who he was. Only how he approached life.

Whether he had his father's approval or not, he wanted to be with Rosie. If they had to be careful to avoid having a baby, then he was prepared to do that too. In fact, even though he knew his father's aim had been to deter him from proposing to Rosie, it had actually helped him to make up his mind. He wanted and needed to have Rosie in his life and he would do whatever it took to have her there.

Whatever it takes.

For himself, he had no qualms about ruining his own reputation. And as for the Hamptons, well, if he was no longer residing at the family ranch, then it wouldn't be a problem for them, would it? Gossip would soon die down and he would just be the prodigal son, the one who went off alone to seek out his own happiness and left his family to move on without him. Exactly what he'd do to make a living, he didn't yet know. He could work the cattle trails to provide for Rosie, or maybe get work at another ranch and send the money back to her. It wouldn't be an ideal life, and he hated the thought of being away from her for long periods of time, but at least he wouldn't have to surrender her then. He'd thought perhaps to take her home to the Hampton ranch where she'd live happily while he worked with the horses, finally giving up his position on the trails to one of his younger brothers. But that couldn't happen now. His father had made that clear. It had been an idealistic and immature young man's dream. Mayhap he actually could save enough to buy a decent amount of land and build up his own business. It would take time, no doubt, but it could be done. Look at what his pa had achieved.

He dusted off his hands and adjusted his Stetson. He would go right now and do it. Head on over to the Duggan homestead and ask Rosie to spend the rest of her life with him, come what may. They could make it work somehow. Although without his Hampton money and inheritance behind him, he wondered what type of a prospect he made. What, exactly, did he have to offer to the woman he loved, other than his heart?

He just had to hope that it would be enough.

* * * *

Rosie finished packing her bag then pushed it under the bed. She would hide it there until she was ready to leave. At first light. That meant that supper this evening would be the last one with her family.

For a while. Not forever.

Nausea surged again, making her feel weak and vulnerable. Who would have thought that emotional turmoil could take such a physical toll? She took slow, deep breaths until the horrid sensation passed then wiped her clammy palms over her apron. She would have to go prepare the evening meal and stick to her usual routine so that no one suspected anything was wrong. Although she doubted that they would. Whilst Kenan was usually quite intuitive about her feelings, being her twin and all, he was currently so wrapped up in his wife and child that he had little thought for anything else. Matthew had been spending a suspicious amount of time in town after meeting Huyana, and Rosie suspected that he was hanging around the place where she stayed, hoping to get the opportunity to speak to her again. Emmett was busy as always, tending to the animals or crafting something out of wood. Just like their father. Emmett had certainly inherited the deceased Mr. Duggan's carpentry skills.

Rosie dabbed her apron above her top lip then over her forehead to clear the perspiration that lay there. She couldn't blame it on the weather. Although spring's progress into summer had been fine so far, they were hardly experiencing a heatwave. *What if...?* She shook her head. A horrible thought, no, she wouldn't entertain it. She was too young for that, surely? She'd heard about the affliction of hot sweats that could affect a woman after a certain age, but wasn't that more likely after forty? Or even later? She was not yet thirty-three. Oh please don't let it be that. Not yet. *But what difference would it make to an aging spinster?*

She stood and shook out her skirts then moved into the living area to find Kenan already washed up and sitting at the table. Catherine was settled in a chair at the hearth, gazing down at Rebecca as she slept in her arms. They were beautiful together and Rosie knew that she would carry their image in her heart, always.

Supper passed in the familiar fashion, with talk and laughter and the warmth of a united family. Kenan announced his plans to extend the homestead now that he had saved enough, and Matthew and Emmett were keen to offer their suggestions. Rosie gazed at each person in turn, capturing their precious outlines, memorizing the sweetness of their voices and their laughter, painfully aware of how much she would miss them.

As she began to clear away the dishes, a knock at the door startled her and she looked across the room, her heart thundering in expectation. She knew who it would be, yet feared the visitor, for she knew that he had the ability to make her reserve crumble.

Kenan opened the door and twilight fell into the room, casting its golden light over the wooden floor as it always did at this time of day. As Kenan stepped back, Joshua's broad frame filled the doorway, his shoulders almost touching the wooden beams at either side. He stood with his legs apart, his large, dusty boots leading up strong shapely legs which were clad in dark material that emphasized his strength and raw masculine virility. Rosie placed a steadying hand on the mantel above the fireplace. She dug her fingers into the wood as if trying to get a physical grip on her emotions.

"Evening, Duggans." Joshua removed his hat. He strode into the room and Kenan patted him on the back as he passed him.

"Are you hungry, Joshua?" Rosie struggled to maintain an even tone.

"No, thank you." He flashed her a smile but it didn't reach his eyes. Their blue appeared dull and he was pale. "I'd like to speak with you, Rosie. If I may?"

The room fell silent. Rosie fumbled with the coffee pot and it clanked as she almost dropped it into the fireplace. Once she had stabilized it on its hook, she turned slowly to face the others. Catherine was trying to distract herself with Rebecca but her brothers all stared at Joshua as if willing him to split fair right there and then.

"Something bothering you, Joshua?" Kenan asked from the bench where he perched, his long legs spread wide, drumming his hands restlessly on his knees.

Joshua pulled himself upright. "Not at all, Kenan. But I'd like to speak to Rosie. Alone. If I may."

Kenan glanced at Rosie and she could see his concern. Was this it? Was this how it would happen? Now? Just when she was about to flee?

"It's fine, Kenan." She inclined her head to indicate her resolve then undid her apron and draped it over the bench. "Shall we go outside, Joshua?"

He held out a hand to allow her to pass and she walked toward the door on wobbly legs. Waiting for Joshua's proposal had been one of the hardest things she had ever endured, but turning it down would be even harder.

Chapter Six

Joshua followed Rosie across the yard, past his tethered horse and out into the surrounding fields. Rosie kept walking until she was wading knee-deep in grass and wild plants.

"You know Kenan will claim all of this land." It wasn't a question. Rosie's voice was flat and gave nothing away about her emotions.

"I'm aware of that. He's spoken to me of his plans."

"He's worked hard to save and to build a life for us all. He's such a good man."

"He is, Rosie. Catherine is a lucky woman."

"And *he's* a lucky man."

Joshua winced at the harshness of Rosie's tone. He had never heard her irritable before and it surprised him. Was she tired of him? Had she reached a point where she had no tenderness left for him? If she had, no wonder. He had taken his time in making an honest woman of her and treated her badly, he could see that now. He had failed her and he deserved a tongue-lashing, if not worse.

"He is that, Rosie. He has everything a man could desire…a beautiful wife and a new baby."

"But what about his reputation?"

"What?" Joshua's heart began to race and he shuddered. What was Rosie talking about? Did she believe that he thought badly of Catherine? He would not judge the girl for her past, whatever it was that had happened had clearly been beyond her control. "There is no stain on his reputation, sweetheart."

Rosie stopped marching and turned to face him.

"You know that's not true but you also know that Kenan doesn't give a damn. He loves Catherine too much to care. What do you want, Joshua?"

With her flashing amber eyes and the color that blazed now in her cheeks, she had a rare kind of beauty. Her cheeks seemed fuller and rounder than before. Her thick ebony hair shone in the evening light. It was pinned at the nape of her neck but a few tendrils had escaped and they danced around her forehead. Standing in the long grass in her faded blue dress, she looked like some kind of warrior woman. It made him long to pull her close, to cover her mouth with his and to make her his forever. But she also made him nervous because he feared that if he did reach out and touch her that she would explode, push him away and break his heart forever.

"Tell me what I've done wrong, Rosie. I need to hear you say it. I know that I should have dealt with our situation before now and I am sorry for it. But I want what I have wanted for months…what I have always wanted, Rosie. I want you to be mine."

She sighed and tore at the wild flowers in front of her, pulling off the heads and tossing them aside.

"It cannot be, Joshua."

The orange-streaked sky collapsed around him and Joshua struggled to stay upright. "Please, Rosie. I'm not sure that you understand. I love you, and I want you to be my wife. I should have made things official a long time ago. I was wrong to wait but I thought that I was doing the right thing..."

Her golden eyes filled with tears and she bit her bottom lip. She seemed to caress him with her gaze then she blinked hard and the beads of liquid burst forth and trickled down her cheeks. She wiped them hurriedly away with the back of her hand.

Joshua stepped closer. "Rosie? Will you marry me?" *Please.* The wind suddenly rushed through the grass and seemed to echo his thoughts...*please...please...please.*

As she shook her head, Joshua's future dispersed before him. She *had* loved him. He had loved her. But he had waited too long. He didn't know exactly why, and he didn't know if Rosie was about to explain, but something had changed and the life he had yearned for would never be realized. The seeds of a future that they had planted together would never come to fruition.

The lovely Rosie Duggan was about to break his heart.

He grabbed hold of her upper arms and pulled her against him. He covered her face with kisses and found her mouth with his own. At first, she resisted, and Joshua wondered if he should stop but suddenly, she softened beneath him and kissed him back.

He was overwhelmed with hunger and need and he reached for the hem of her skirt and lifted it then pushed his hand between her thighs. She was wet already. He had to take her, to have her before he lost her forever.

He stroked her sex, parting her folds, then slipped two fingers inside her. As he touched her like that, she trembled and climaxed quickly.

Joshua turned her around and lowered her to her knees. As he lifted her skirt again, she leaned forward and rested on her hands, knowing instinctively what he was about to do. He loosened his trousers and freed his cock then pushed into her in one go. Her flesh was hot and tight around him and he took her hard and fast, erupting into her quickly with a groan.

When his erection began to wane, he slid out of her and pressed her to his chest, his heart thundering from his climax and also from fear. He could not bear to hear what he feared she was about to say.

Being cold toward Joshua was the hardest thing Rosie had ever done but she forced herself to do it. To be strong. She slipped out of his arms and righted her clothing.

"We cannot be together, Joshua." She said it again, to convince herself as much as him, as she stood and took a step backward.

"But why, sweetheart?"

"You do not love me, Joshua. Not really."

"That's not true, Rosie. Not true at all." Joshua stood too.

"It's taken you a long time to propose, and I fear that you're doing it out of sympathy or a sense of duty...because of this." She gestured at them both.

"No, Rosie, no." His face crumpled and Rosie wrapped her arms around her waist to prevent herself from rushing forward and hugging him. In the long run, this would be for the best. Right now, it burned her to the core, but they would survive and Joshua would move on. As he should. As they both should.

But Rosie would still go away for a while, just to make sure.

"What we had was...good while it lasted. But I..." *Can I really say it?* "I don't love you either." The words nearly choked her. *So untrue. Such awful lies.* But it was the only thing that would make him leave and she knew it.

Joshua frowned and whispered her words over and over as if trying to accept them. He kept shaking his head and flexing his hands. She wondered briefly, how far would a desperate man go? But if she didn't release Joshua now, then Dylan Hampton might wreak a far worse revenge, and he would certainly cut his own son out of his life. She couldn't see that happen.

"It's best you go now. Go on home." She waved a hand in a shooing motion. "Best you do."

She turned on her heel and began to stride toward the house. The long grass seemed to reach out to her as if trying to stop her, to hold her back so that she couldn't break two hearts. But she forced her legs on in spite of the burning of her calf muscles, in spite of the searing pain in her chest and the sour bile in her throat.

"Rosie."

His whisper followed her on the breeze and though she willed herself not to glance back, she did.

"I do love you, Rosie, and I'll prove it to you. And I know you love me too."

"No, Joshua, I don't. Not at all. Now go on home and don't come back. I don't ever want to see you again."

Free of the long grass, she hurried on, tears coursing down her cheeks and her chest heaving with pain, even as Joshua's seed trickled down her thighs.

It was for the best and she knew it. Best for everyone involved.

So why didn't it feel like it?

Chapter Seven

Rosie squinted as she stepped off the stagecoach and into the bright afternoon sunlight. It had been a difficult morning but she had made it to her destination. She pulled her shawl tightly around her shoulders then followed the procession of people away from the raised platform that had been installed to ease the arrival and departure of the stages, and off toward the town.

Her legs shook beneath her plain black skirts and she had a strange feeling in her stomach. It was as if a hard ball of clay had settled there. But every so often, it would roll over and create the most unsettling fluttering. She had to admit that she was actually somewhat excited. Which she had not expected. Here she was, setting out into the world alone, unchaperoned — for the first time ever — and she felt strangely liberated. It was completely unforeseen.

The people in front of her shuffled along and she was glad of their slowness, for it gave her the opportunity to look around and to get her bearings. The first thing she needed to do was find somewhere to stay. Then she would need to find employment. In the dead of night whilst her family slept, though it had made her heart ache to do it, she had lifted the floorboards beneath the wooden table in the homestead and removed some of Kenan's savings. She knew where he kept the money because he'd had no reason to hide it from her. *Until now.* She could not bear to think of what he would say when he realized that it had gone and that his own twin was a thief who had taken the money he'd sweated and toiled to save. He had aimed to use it to create a better future for his wife, child and siblings. She had left a note promising that she would pay him back just as soon as she was earning but she still felt the noose of her betrayal chafing at the tender flesh of her throat.

With any luck, he would not even find out that it was gone and she could send it to him with any extra that she had to spare. The fear that she might not be able to do so made her suddenly aware of the heat of the spring afternoon, and tiny beads of perspiration rolled down her chest and soaked into her chemise where it was compressed by her corset.

As the queue dispersed and folks wandered off through the town in all directions, Rosie looked both ways. Up or down? She could make out houses, shops, saloons, a stable and a post office. The dusty main street of Nevada City was busy as people made purchases or chatted about the weather and horses trotted up and down, guided by businessmen and cowboys and pulling carts laden with produce. She had taken the stagecoach from Virginia City to Nevada City, knowing that her brothers frequented the former location too often for her to avoid discovery. But here, she hoped to avoid being found.

It was far enough away but not too far as to cause her to panic.

"Excuse me, ma'am, may I be of assistance?" Rosie froze. The man's voice was deep and laced with an unfamiliar accent. She turned cautiously to face him and breathed a sigh of relief.

"You may if you know where I can find a place to stay and perhaps some form of employment, sir." She offered a thin smile to the very short man in front of her. He was hunched over, which obviously made him appear shorter than he actually was, and she wondered at his affliction. His brown suit was heavily soiled, and whenever he moved, it gave off a sour, musty aroma that left Rosie struggling not to gag.

"There's the Nevada City Hotel. Though I'm not sure that they've got vacancies, ma'am." The man blinked quickly then lifted his Stetson and raked a grubby hand through his damp, dark hair. "However, I could take ya to see Mrs. Appleby. She takes in boarders for a small fee and she's very nice indeed."

Rosie chewed her lip. Hotel or boarding house. She glanced at the man and fought the urge to recoil as he spat out a lump of brown phlegm. It landed at her side, just missing the hem of her skirt. What if this man was a degenerate, intent on leading young women astray as soon as they arrived at Nevada City? What if…?

"You want my help or not, ma'am? See, there'll be another stage in soon and I need the money from helping folks out. I ain't real good for much else." His cheeks flushed and he dropped his gaze to the ground. Rosie gasped. How could she have been so insensitive? He was clearly hunched over because of a distortion of his spine. *The poor man.*

"Yes, please, sir. I would like to meet this Mrs. Appleby. If I may."

He doffed his hat then reached for her bag. Rosie hugged it to her chest. Though Kenan's money was wrapped in linen and tucked beneath her corset, she did not feel comfortable handing the man her meager possessions. *Just in case.* She had a few coins tucked into her left glove which she would use to pay the man when she was safely escorted to the boarding house.

He shrugged as if unsurprised at her reluctance to part with her belongings. "This way then."

He limped off along the street and Rosie followed him, surprised at how quickly he moved in spite of his disability. She was acutely aware of the stares that she attracted as she walked. She had hoped that the somber black gown and shawl with a plain black bonnet would spare her too much interest and that folks would suspect that she was the widow of some recently deceased miner, but she now recalled Kenan and Matthew talking about how the population of Nevada City had dwindled over the last few years as miners moved on to seek out gold pockets elsewhere. So, like all newcomers, she was bound to attract attention, even in widow's weeds.

Her guide stopped suddenly in front of a wooden-fronted building that appeared to be built onto the side of another. Though the exterior was somewhat shabby, the windows were clean and had frilled pink curtains at the sides. Perhaps this wouldn't be so bad. A sudden wave of homesickness washed over her for the cozy homestead and the familiar landscape she had left just that morning.

"You want me to knock and speak to Mrs. Appleby for ya?" The man tilted his head to one side as he waited for an answer. Rosie saw one of the curtains twitch and realized that someone inside must be curious about her intentions.

She slid a finger into her glove and shook her head. "No. Thank you. You've been very kind."

She held out her hand and the man approached her. She dropped a few coins into his palm and had to bite back a protest as he lifted them to his mouth and bit them in turn. Apparently satisfied, he pocketed the money then nodded at Rosie before loping off in the direction they had come. He turned once, as if to check that she was still there, and she raised her hand and smiled but he merely nodded then continued on his way.

Rosie took a shaky breath. So here she was. Alone in a strange town. About to ask a stranger if she could lodge with her. But wasn't that what other folks did? Especially young women new to an area. Surely it was better than walking into a hotel alone? She shivered. What was Joshua doing now? Would Kenan have informed him about her disappearance or would he have suspected him of eloping with Rosie? Would Joshua be hurt or relieved that she was gone?

Just as grief and guilt threatened to consume her, the front door of the house swung open and a buxom woman with fat pink cheeks and golden sausage curls stepped onto the porch. Rosie's quick perusal suggested that she was about her age, but with all that makeup on, it was hard to tell.

"Now what's a strange young lady doing standing outside my house on such a hot afternoon? The sun will surely destroy your fair complexion." She frowned but her green eyes danced with mischief.

"I...uh... Do you happen to have a spare room, ma'am? I was brought here by a man..." She gestured at the street but her guide was nowhere to be seen. Rosie shifted her bag to her other arm and held out her right hand. "My name is Rosie. Rosie Duggan."

The woman opened her mouth and let out a belly laugh that made her blonde curls shake. "I'm sure you are, sweeting, and I'm Queen Cleopatra! Sure I have room for a young lady like yourself. Come on in and let's get ya settled afore folks round here start pestering ya." She pointed behind Rosie and whispered, "Don't turn round honey. Ya don't wanna give them randy varmints anymore reason ta get excited than y'already have."

With that, she ushered Rosie into a shadowy hallway that smelled of stale bacon and tobacco smoke and bolted the door behind them.

* * * *

Joshua lifted his head from the paperwork spread over the long kitchen table. He'd been going through some figures for his father, trying to work out where they could cut costs, but his heart hadn't been in it. Over and over again, he heard Rosie's last words to him and his heart broke anew... *I don't ever want to see you again.*

He tried to find some salvation in the memory, some trace of affection on her face as she'd looked at him, but there had been nothing there, nothing to offer him hope. Just sadness and a coldness—a distance he had never seen before. As he'd tried to work out the figures, the numbers had seemed to dance across the pages before him, taunting him for his inability to make the woman he loved happy. He'd been about to give up when a commotion erupted outside. He pushed to his feet and hurried into the main room of the ranch and peered out of the window.

Kenan Duggan was trying to push past his brothers Billy and Christopher, and yelling at them as they refused to let go of his arms. Kenan's face was bright red and his hat had fallen off and now rolled around on the ground in front of him. What could be wrong?

Rosie!

Joshua flung open the door and ran onto the porch. "What is it?"

"You!" Kenan shouted. "It's all your fault. You spent so long dallying and leading my sister a merry dance that she's upped and left. That poor girl had a broken heart and all because of you." He made a fresh attempt to get past the Hampton brothers but they held him fast, which couldn't have been easy, as he was a big man. He clenched his fists repeatedly and Joshua knew exactly what Kenan would do to him if he got away from Billy and Christopher.

Joshua walked toward Kenan and held his hands up. "I don't know what you're talking about, Kenan. What do you mean she's upped and left? Rosie's gone?" Panic filled his chest and he raked his hands through his hair. "*Where* has she gone?"

"I don't know." Kenan's face crumpled for a moment before he regained control. "She took a few things and went while we were sleeping. I thought at first that she might have come here, but then judging by the state of her after you left last night, I doubt that she'd ever want to see your face again. But I'd hoped that you might have some idea, that she gave you some clue about where she was headed."

Joshua shook his head. "I had no idea that she'd run off. None at all. She said nothing last night that would suggest that she intended leaving."

"What's going on here, Joshua?" Billy asked as he let go of Kenan's arm but remained close to him, eyeing him cautiously.

Joshua looked at his younger brother. Apart from his parents, he wasn't sure that his family knew about his feelings for Rosie. He'd kept his mouth shut, trying to find the right time to tell them all. His gut churned as he realized that he might never get that chance now. Why had he waited? Why had he been such a cowardly, hesitant fool?

"I'm in love with Rosie Duggan and I want to marry her."

"What?" Kenan frowned at him and Billy and Christopher paused for a moment then began slapping him on the back and congratulating him.

"I love her, Kenan, and last night I asked her to be my wife."

"You did? At last! Then why in the hell has she run off?" Kenan took his Stetson from Christopher and brushed the dust off it. "Surely, you two should be celebrating not—"

"She turned me down."

"Why in the hell would she do that?" Kenan stared from one Hampton brother to another. "It's clear that she loves you, too. So why would she reject you?"

"She had her reasons." Joshua hung his head. He was too ashamed to say them out loud here, in front of Rosie's brother and his own. If anything happened to her, he would never forgive himself. "Kenan, I love Rosie with all of my heart and I'll search high and low for her. I'll find her, I swear. If it takes the rest of my life."

Kenan shook his head. "No, you won't."

"Whadda ya mean?" Joshua could not bear the thought of staying at his father's ranch and pretending that he'd never known Rosie, that he wasn't desperate to know that she was safe and well. Anything could happen to a woman out there, alone. Anything. He shuddered at the thought of it. The country was so dangerous and Rosie was so good and innocent — used to being protected. She'd never survive without her family.

"What I mean...brother" — Kenan reached out and took hold of Joshua's shoulder — "is that *we* will find her. Together."

Joshua swallowed hard. He didn't deserve this kindness from Kenan. But then he didn't deserve Rosie's love. Never had done. But he'd do everything he could to bring her home safely. Then he'd do the right thing and make sure that she knew how much he loved her. Even if she didn't want him, he'd make sure that she never wanted for anything ever again.

And his mother and father could go to hell.

Chapter Eight

Rosie perched on the edge of the bed in the small room at Mrs. Appleby's boarding house. The late afternoon sunlight shone across the wooden floor and made the dust in the air sparkle. Rosie's small patchwork bag containing the few possessions she'd packed lay at her feet, a poignant reminder that it was all she possessed in the world and of the family she had left behind.

Mrs. Appleby fussed around, showing Rosie where to find extra blankets and explaining how she ran the house. It seemed that she had three young ladies currently boarding with her and that they all paid her a small cash fee as well as helping out around the house. Rosie was confused by the reference to gentlemen callers who apparently arrived at all times of the day and night. Why on earth would a respectable woman allow her boarders to indulge in such inappropriate behavior? At the edges of Rosie's mind, the truth lurked dark and intriguing, yet she had far more important concerns to deal with, so she pushed her questions away.

"Will you come downstairs with me and help to prepare dinner, dear?" Mrs. Appleby offered her broad and cheery smile. Rosie noted for the first time that the woman's dress was rather low-cut and slightly grubby around the hem where her petticoats were exposed in what appeared to be a deliberate fashion. Was this how women dressed in Nevada City then? Was it a new fashion that had made its way from New York? It reminded her of the whores she'd seen in Virginia City as they paraded up and down the porches of the establishments where they resided. Yet they wore far less than Mrs. Appleby and she had no reason to suspect that this woman was a whore. Tiredness and the heat must be affecting her judgment.

"Rosie, dear? Are you coming?"

Rosie wanted to decline, to tell the older woman that she had a headache and needed to rest, but she didn't want to cause offense. Her temples throbbed and her thoughts seemed to be running into one another so quickly that she felt she would faint. She needed some time, even just ten minutes, to clear her mind. She was overcome by a sudden longing for the wide open space of the Montana sky and the endless horizon that stretched out around the Duggan homestead. The town of Nevada City felt small, dirty and claustrophobic and she tried to stifle a sense of rising panic.

"Yes, Mrs. Appleby. I will come down. But would you mind if I just freshen up? The stagecoach was crowded and I'm a trifle warm." She longed to retrieve Kenan's money from beneath her corset and to be alone with her thoughts. Her stays seemed even more restricting than usual and her ribs felt sore and bruised, as if damaged by her broken heart.

Where was Joshua now? Would he even care that she had gone?

"Of course, Rosie, but don't be long!" Mrs. Appleby wagged a fat finger at her then exited the room, leaving the mixed aroma of sweat and rosewater in her wake.

Rosie quickly removed Kenan's cash from its hiding place then tucked it under her mattress. It should be safe there. As long as no one came snooping around. But what reason would they have to look under her mattress?

She crossed the small space to the dresser and filled the pewter bowl with water from the pitcher then washed her face. Her cheeks burned and she wondered if she had some sort of fever. Imagine that—leaving home and hiding out in a strange town only to develop smallpox or some other awful infection—then dying alone, away from those she loved. What if she never saw them all again? They would wonder what had happened to her as they did when Catherine had disappeared. They would never give up hope. The Duggans never did. The thought choked her and she leaned forward, bile rising suddenly. Perhaps the nausea she'd been experiencing was a warning of some other horrid disease. Perhaps her time in this world was limited.

Stop it right now, Rosie Duggan! You are a sensible and mature woman and you need to pull yourself together. You will see your family again – when things have settled down.

She dried her face on the clean cloth provided and tidied her hair using the small oval looking glass that hung on a nail above the dresser. Even though the surface of the mirror was misty, it was like staring at a stranger. Apart from the dark red blotches on her cheeks, which hinted at a fever, she was so ashen-faced that she could have been a ghost, and the dark hollows beneath her eyes did little to help that. Yet her face still seemed fuller than usual and her gaze emitted a glow, as if releasing a luminescence from within. The infection must be clouding her brain.

As must her heartbreak. This would not do. She had made her decision and for all the right reasons. She had to learn to accept and move on. She had done the decent thing.

So why was it so difficult?

* * * *

Downstairs, Rosie sat at the worn wooden kitchen table and peeled potatoes. Their starch turned her hands white but she found the everyday activity comforting. Wherever she was, whoever she was with, folks still needed potatoes peeling.

Mrs. Appleby hummed as she fried chunks of meat and slices of onion over the large open fire, and two other young women clattered about, trying to make themselves useful but invariably getting in each other's way. In spite of her emotional turmoil, Rosie couldn't help smiling. It was like being at a show, watching these heavily made-up women in their garish dresses — for the other women's garments were far more daring than Mrs. Appleby's — as they attempted to complete everyday household tasks. She was so used to preparing meals alone, or with Catherine helping quietly, that the noise and bustle of the Appleby kitchen was quite overwhelming.

"So…Rosie, ya said ya name is?" The tiny brunette known as Fennella leaned over the table and stared hard. Rosie tried to avert her eyes from the woman's exposed cleavage but it was difficult to avoid it when her bosoms were almost resting on the tabletop.

My, they do wear their dresses low-cut here.

"That's right. My name actually is Rosie." She held Fennella's gaze. Why did they all seem to think it was a fake name?

"Yeah and my real name is Fennella." The girl cackled and slapped her hand on her thigh. "Okay then...*Rosie*...so what are ya doing in Nevada City?"

"I needed a...change of scenery to deal with my...my loss." Rosie felt her cheeks flame at the misinformation. Sure she was grieving, but not for a dead husband—for one who had never been.

"You a widow?" Fennella studied her nails as if disinterested now.

Rosie nodded.

"Likely story." The girl, that was what she must have been for she appeared no older than seventeen, raised an eyebrow as she looked Rosie over. "No wedding ring, see?"

Rosie pulled her left hand into her lap and rubbed at her naked ring finger. No. The girl was right. No wedding ring. *Fool!*

"So you gonna explain what you're doing in Nevada City or not?"

Rosie blinked rapidly, trying to hold the ready tears at bay. Fennella was so harsh, so direct. Rosie was not used to dealing with such people and she wished that she could go home. Immediately. But that couldn't happen. As she breathed deeply, trying to regain her composure, black spots swam before her and she closed them for a moment.

Keep calm, keep still, it will pass.

When Rosie opened her eyes again, she saw that she had a captive audience of three. They stared down at her like a trio of hungry wolves, their mouths gaping and their teeth exposed. She shuddered.

Fennella was the first to pounce. "How far along are ya?"

"What?" Rosie dropped the knife she'd been peeling potatoes with and straightened her back. She rubbed her sticky hands together, uncomfortably aware now of the starch drying on her skin. "I don't understand what you mean."

Did the girl know that she had left home? Was she asking how long Rosie had been running? She didn't want anyone to know. Her story was that she was recently widowed and taking some time away from home to deal with her grief. That was the façade she wanted to maintain, even if some folks doubted its sincerity. The last thing she wanted was a barrage of questions from virtual strangers.

"I mean, how long since your last bleed?"

Rosie gasped and covered her chest with her hands. How could the girl be so coarse?

"She doesn't know." Mrs. Appleby gestured at Rosie with her knife. "She has no idea what you're talking about."

Rosie looked from one face to another. The other young woman, Helen, placed her work reddened hands on the tabletop. Helen might be lodging with Mrs. Appleby now but it was clear that she had worked hard in the past, maybe not even that long ago. Had it been her parents who had set her toiling at their farm or had she been taken in by a rancher as a low-paid picker? "Rosie, what Fennella meant was, when did you see your last course? Was it this month?"

Rosie tore her eyes from Helen's hands. Shame washed over her. Then realization dawned. She struggled to swallow. "No..." She shook her head. "No. No. No."

"Denying it won't do any good, sweetheart." Mrs. Appleby walked around the table and squeezed Rosie's shoulder. "You're expecting or I'm a virgin." She snorted at that and the other two joined her.

Rosie stood and backed away from the table. She wrung her hands together and sucked in her cheeks. Expecting? A child? Her?

"But... How is it possible?"

"I've been around a while, Rosie, dear and seen a lot. Seen many a young woman carrying a child she didn't want and running away to avoid the scandal. That's what it is with you, right? You fall for a married man and let him get his greasy mitts on yer? Or did ya let a handsome young stallion take yer over his saddle?"

Rosie shook her head and ran a hand over her stomach. It was flat beneath her corset. Almost.

"Have you been feeling queasy lately, honey?" Fennella asked, suddenly kind.

Rosie chewed her lip.

"Have your breasts ached more than usual when you remove your corset?" Mrs. Appleby resumed squeezing Rosie's shoulder.

Rosie nodded. "But only the past few weeks... Maybe two or three." They had been heavy and she had been aware of a dull ache that afflicted them when she first sat up in the mornings and when she removed her corset in the evenings.

"So you're a few months in is all." Mrs. Appleby adjusted her huge bosom. "I know someone who can help you with that—if you don't want to keep the child, that is."

Rosie looked at the three women in turn, registering the understanding on their faces. They weren't judging her as she had first thought, but they were so matter of fact about it too. As if this happened all the time.

But it probably does. To them.

"Help me with it?"

"Yes, ya know. Help you to get rid of it. I mean, you can't possibly be thinking of keeping it, dear." Mrs. Appleby spoke as calmly, as if she was talking about throwing away an old shawl or a stained rag.

Get rid of it?

"Have you...?" Rosie couldn't finish her question. It was inappropriate. Horror washed over her.

"Have I ever had to get rid of a child?" Rosie's landlady raised her fair eyebrows. "More than I care to count, dear."

So these poor women conceived babies that they didn't want then had them removed from their bodies as casually as performing any other ablution. How could this be right? Or was Rosie just too sheltered to know what really went on in the world?

"But what about your husbands?" Rosie had to ask, though she had an inkling that she already knew the answer.

The three women cackled until they were red-faced and sweaty.

"Husbands?" Mrs. Appleby rubbed her greasy forehead. "We have no men to keep us, sweeting. Men pay us for our time but we have no husbands. Thank the Lord! Oh, you're an innocent one, ya are! I'm thinking that old Danny read you wrongly when he brought ya here. What do ya think, girls?"

Fennella and Helen grinned their agreement.

"You have been misled, my dear, and some nasty man took advantage, didn't he?" Mrs. Appleby shook her head and her jowls wobbled. "Don't you worry, Rosie. Mrs. Appleby will take care of ya now."

As her landlady returned to frying steak and Fennella and Helen took over the potato peeling, Rosie quietly left the heat of the kitchen. Her hands trembled uncontrollably and her legs shook beneath her skirts.

If there was such a place as hell, then she was surely in it. She was carrying Joshua's child. She had not thought for a minute that it was possible. She'd known how it could happen but with her age and — Oh, she had been a fool. She had taken her pleasure with the man she loved and now she would have to pay the biggest price of all. For she had refused Joshua's proposal for sound reasons. She had been thinking of him and his family and what she did not want to put him through. Yet now, here she was, with a babe in her belly and no prospects for the future at all. How could she bring a child into the world to be a shameful bastard?

Yet how could she destroy that precious, tiny life before it had even begun?

Chapter Nine

Joshua sat on the Duggan porch and swirled coffee around his mouth. He tapped his feet in turn, his knees bouncing along with them. Kenan had decided that they would leave at first light, but the thought of waiting tortured him. He was so agitated, he felt as if it would be better to be crushed in a stampede than going through such anxiety about the woman he loved. At least if he could get moving, he'd feel like he was doing something.

He should have protected Rosie and given her love and security before things got this far.

He was responsible for this, and he would never forgive himself if anything happened to her. The thought that someone might take advantage of her turned him cold yet filled him with a white-hot rage. If anyone so much as harmed a hair on her sweet head he'd—

"You all right?"

Joshua glanced behind him to see Catherine. She gestured at the step beside him. "Mind if I sit down?"

"Go ahead." He shrugged. He didn't know that he could focus on conversation right now.

"How are you feeling?" Catherine's big green eyes glowed in the twilight. Joshua found himself suddenly wanting to speak to her, to try to explain himself, to convey just how miserable he was that things had gone so wrong.

"Just awful, ma'am."

"Oh, Joshua. Please call me Catherine. There's no need for 'ma'am' with me. It's so formal and it makes me feel so old."

He smiled. Catherine was a good woman, and it was hard to see how anyone could think badly of her.

"Thank you, Catherine."

"You're worried sick right now, aren't you?"

He nodded. "I can't believe she's gone, that she isn't inside making dinner or fussing around one of you. I'm fair stewing in my own juices 'cos of how she must've been hurting to run off like that. Why didn't I prevent this? I just can't accept that she's not here."

"Me either. Rosie is a rare breed of woman. She's so sweet and kind. Even though she's just a few years older, she's like a mother to me. It's strange." Catherine pushed her red hair over her shoulders. "And she's been such a help with the little one." Catherine bit her lip and Joshua could see that she was holding back her own distress.

"I know that," Joshua replied. "Rosie adores her niece." The image of Rosie holding the baby in her arms and gazing at her with that look that was warm, loving and needy all at once made his chest ache. He hoped to see her holding their own child one day, he was more certain of that now than ever before.

"You have to bring her back, Joshua. She loves you. As much as a woman can love a man."

The pain in Joshua's throat threatened to cut off his air supply altogether.

"I love her, too."

"So bring her back and do the right thing by her." Catherine got up off the step. "You're the only one with the power to change her mind. So go do it."

"I will," Joshua whispered as Catherine disappeared into the house. "I will."

* * * *

Rosie trembled as Mrs. Appleby led her past buildings, yards and animal pens before arriving at the scruffy shack. Rosie wasn't sure that she'd be able to find her way out again if her landlady left her there. Evidently, the woman who lodged at the ramshackle hut did not want to be visible from the main thoroughfare, or at all easy to locate. Which was understandable given her line of business.

The killing of innocents.

Now stop it! You have no other choice, Rosie, and neither do the other poor women who come here seeking assistance. A woman's options are limited.

The breakfast that Mrs. Appleby had insisted she eat now sat heavy in her stomach and threatened to make a reappearance at any moment. She swallowed hard repeatedly, willing it to stay in place.

They entered the small, dark space and Mrs. Appleby pointed at a narrow pine table against the rear wall. "Go lie on that table there and she'll examine ya."

Rosie looked from the table to her landlady's face and back again. "Really?"

"Yes. Now hurry up. We don't want to be hanging around here any longer than we have ta." Mrs.

Appleby took a seat next to the front door and pulled some sewing from her bag.

Rosie perched on the edge then lifted her legs up and lay down. She spread out her black skirts and waited. She crossed then uncrossed her ankles. Was this the right thing to do? Could she really go through with it?

A curtain moved in the corner of the room and a woman appeared. Rosie eyed her from her vulnerable position. Mrs. Appleby had warned her that the midwife's appearance was shocking but that she wasn't to mention it. Susanna, as she was known, had apparently wandered off as a child and been taken in by the Indians. During her time with them, they had tattooed her cheeks and chin with markings befitting her status in their tribe. Years later, Susanna had been 'rescued' by a band of soldiers and returned to civilization. Mrs. Appleby had shaken her head as she'd said 'rescued', implying that Susanna had in fact been taken from her adopted family against her will. When the soldiers had tried to make Susanna talk, to turn her to into some sort of exhibit or entertainment to regale them with the tales of her kidnapping and abuse — more head shaking from Mrs. Appleby — she'd cut out her own tongue. Mrs. Appleby seemed to believe that it was something to do with a code of honor that had been instilled into the woman. Whatever her reasons, she must have been pretty desperate to resort to such measures. How cruel it had been to take her away from her family, the people she knew and loved, just to return her to life as a white woman where she was now classed as no better than the soiled doves. Mayhap even lower than the women she helped. Desperate indeed.

As you are now. But it's not your tongue that will be cut out.

As Rosie watched the woman washing her hands, then preparing something in a small bowl which she ground into a paste, she felt no horror or revulsion. Just compassion. How awful to be so desperate that you cut out your own tongue just to avoid talking. Was it her Indian family who were to blame or the soldiers who tried to use her as a showpiece? Rosie knew that the truth was not as straightforward as some might believe, and she admired Mrs. Appleby's understanding of this fact. But then, her landlady had probably seen and heard a lot during her time.

Susanna approached Rosie and she tried to still her trembling but her body refused to obey—her wanton body, the weak flesh that had led her astray and gotten her into this mess. *Along with your foolish heart.*

Susanna stopped at Rosie's side and took hold of her wrist. She held it tightly just below the bone and waited. Rosie held her breath. After what seemed like an eternity, Susanna released Rosie's hand then motioned that Rosie should lift her skirts.

Shame crawled over Rosie. How could she expose herself here in front of this stranger?

"Don't be afraid, Rosie. Susanna knows what she's doing, and she's seen plenty of cunnies before."

Rosie shuddered at Mrs. Appleby's muttered words, but did as she suggested. She stared at the dusty beams of the ceiling and tried to think about something else, something other than the small, dexterous hands that Susanna ran over her stomach, smoothing, pressing and exploring. She had never had another woman touch her before, and although the examination was clearly an assessment of her pregnancy, it made her uncomfortable all the same.

"So?" Mrs. Appleby stood next to Susanna. "How far along is she?"

Rosie watched the tattooed woman raise her hands then point to her fingers.

"Ah…almost three months in. As I suspected. So it'll still be small, dear, and easy enough to deliver."

Rosie hurriedly pushed her skirts down and sat up. She had seen Catherine's baby emerge into the world, a few weeks early but healthy and strong. Could she really force her own child to make an early entrance, one that would surely destroy its chances of survival? Would it be alive as it was born? Or would they give her something to stop its heart before she gave birth? This could be the only child she would ever conceive.

She wiped at the tears that trickled down her cheeks. She was expected to destroy the thing she had longed for, yearned for, dreamed of. To murder the living being that came from her coupling with Joshua in love, in passion and in trust.

As she stood, she caught Susanna watching her intently. The woman's brown eyes were filled with something warm and kind. *Compassion.* And it hurt to see it. For right now, Rosie didn't feel that she deserved it. She didn't deserve it at all.

* * * *

Joshua rode into Virginia City at Kenan Duggan's side. Matthew and Emmett had remained at the homestead to watch over Catherine and the baby, as well as to keep things in order there.

"So where do you think we should start?" Kenan gestured at the town.

"Where would Rosie be likely to go? Does she know anyone here?"

"She's acquainted with a few folks, but she didn't have any close friends here," Kenan replied. "Guess we just work our way around and ask if anyone has seen her. You start at the far end, I'll start at the saloon and we can meet up in the middle."

"Sounds good to me." Joshua dug his heels into his mare.

By noon, they had asked everyone they could find if they'd seen Rosie but it seemed that nobody had. Joshua knew that with her slender frame, amber eyes and sleek black hair, she'd be bound to attract attention. The thought made his guts churn.

"She can't have just vanished," Kenan muttered, a small muscle in his jaw twitching as he watched the people milling along the busy main street. "I can't believe I'm going through this again. First Catherine and now Rosie."

Vanished. The word pierced Joshua's chest like an arrow. She might well have vanished. Could be that someone had taken her. Like Catherine, who had been missing for over two years. This must be really hard for Kenan. First his intended, and now his twin sister. And as for Joshua himself...how would he cope without Rosie? How could he live knowing that she was out there somewhere, maybe hurt, scared, alone and wanting him to rescue her?

"Could be she took the stagecoach." Joshua thought it was unlikely but who knew how desperate Rosie had been. Perhaps she even suspected that they'd come looking for her so she'd decided to go farther away. *Perhaps. Please let it be that.* The alternatives were too awful to contemplate. He was helpless and it wasn't a feeling he liked at all.

"So we try the next town?" Kenan's eyes were screwed up against the sun glare but even so, Joshua could see the pain etched on his face. The worry seemed to have aged him overnight and this morning he was unshaven and unkempt. Not like Kenan at all.

"Yeah. Let's try Nevada City," Joshua replied.

All he could do was hope that they would find Rosie there. If she'd gone even farther, their chances of locating her would get slimmer. It was a dangerous world and the longer Rosie was out there alone, the higher the possibility that she would get hurt. A sensation built inside him like some sort of internal tornado. It picked up strength and speed and he feared that it would burst out of his mouth in a deafening roar if he didn't find Rosie soon. He *had* to keep moving, *had* to believe that this would have a good outcome.

"We will do, but I think we should return to the homestead first. She might have come back." Kenan chewed at his lip.

"She might have. In fact, she most probably has!" Joshua allowed hope to bubble in his belly. The idea of returning to the homestead to find Rosie there lifted his heart and made it soar into the clouds. If they got back to find his beloved there, he would grab hold of her and never, ever let her go. He would darned well make her marry him and no more nonsense about it. She was his and they belonged together.

The thought put energy into his body and he spurred his horse onward. They had to get to back to the homestead as quickly as possible. He ached to hold his woman in his arms, to know that she was safe and well. The thought that she might not be there danced ominously at the back of his mind and he willed it to quiet down. If she wasn't at home, then they would head out to the next town and the next until they found her. Joshua knew that he would never give up. So a trip to Nevada City was a possibility.

Rosie's life might depend upon it. *His* life depended upon finding her.

But until he knew if she was at the homestead, he would put his fears on hold.

Chapter Ten

Rosie rolled over on the narrow bed. She'd been unable to fall asleep until the early hours and had endured a restless night. The sunlight stealing through the curtains told her that it was past noon. No one at Mrs. Appleby's had tried to wake her, but she suspected that they were all still asleep. Judging by their noisy nocturnal activities, they would need to rest until well into the afternoon. Throughout the night, Rosie had heard a variety of male visitors coming and going, their heavy footsteps on the stairs and their muffled grunts and groans in the adjacent rooms were difficult to ignore. She had lain in her bed, stiff with fear that one of the men might try her door. But she had been spared that indignity.

Rosie sat up and threw her legs over the edge of the straw mattress. There it was again—the horrible queasy feeling. But now she knew why she was experiencing it. Catherine had spoken of it during her pregnancy, but it had ceased when she reached her four month mark and she had bloomed as her body had swelled. Rosie hunched over and dry wretched.

Her own body would know no such joy. It would never swell with fertility and femininity. It would never stretch as the child grew inside her or produce milk to feed that child.

She glanced at the dresser. It was still there. That small jar which held the concoction prepared by Susanna. The poison that would destroy the baby she had created with Joshua.

Susanna had gestured to Mrs. Appleby how and when Rosie should ingest the paste, but it was clear that Mrs. Appleby was familiar with the routine, that she had taken it herself and knew how it would work. As they had left the small, gloomy cabin, Susanna had grabbed Rosie's arm and stared at her. It had unnerved Rosie, the intensity in the brown eyes and the tight pinching of the woman's fingers in her sensitive flesh. The midwife had pointed at Rosie's stomach and at her arms and made a rocking motion whilst smiling. Rosie shook her head in confusion, so Susanna had mimed placing the invisible a baby on the ground then run her fingers down her cheeks to suggest tears.

"She's telling you to be sure before you do this," Mrs. Appleby had explained. "Because once that baby's out, you can't change what you've done. She seems to think that you're not certain about this, dear. You must be. Otherwise…"

Otherwise. But there was no otherwise. No alternative. Rosie had gotten herself in the family way and had no husband to support her. Though she knew in her heart that Kenan and Catherine would help her, no matter what, she dared not bring the shame of a bastard child to the Duggan homestead. They had all endured enough over recent years, and she would not add to their troubles. If she did this now, got rid of the child and spared it from a life that would certainly be harsh and definitely unfair, then she could return to her family and remain there, placing each day between her and the terrible knowledge of what she had done. Keeping it to herself so that nobody else ever had to know about it.

This was the right thing to do. Wasn't it?

It will be my deep, dark secret. My pain. My sacrifice. My shame.

She stood and reached out to the dresser then picked up the small jar and removed the lid. As she raised her trembling hand, she took a deep breath. This was the best thing to do in a bad situation. She had made the mess, so it was up to her to clean it up.

Even if it broke her heart.

* * * *

Joshua tethered his horse next to Kenan's outside the Nevada City General Store. The main street was quiet in the late afternoon, apart from a few miners on their way to wash up.

"I'm gonna ask inside if anyone has seen Rosie. You keep an eye on the horses. I'm not sure about this place. It don't feel right."

Joshua nodded at Kenan. He knew what he meant. They were used to Virginia City, as well as other cattle towns that they'd stopped in whilst herding his father's prized beasts along the trails, but there had been trouble in Nevada City a while back and it felt as if folks were still recovering. There was an edge to the place that he didn't like. It made the hairs on the back of his neck stand up and he was tense, ready to spring into action if necessary.

What if Rosie was here? His stomach churned. She might well have gotten hurt in a place like this. If anyone had laid their hands on her then he'd just…

Kenan appeared at his side. "Man in there said there was a stagecoach came in day before yesterday. Said there were a few young women on it…his son's friend commented on them being comely and all. I asked if they'd said anything about a slim, black-haired woman and he called his son from out the back. He seemed to recall a woman fitting Rosie's description – actually claimed she resembled me somewhat – but said…"

"What is it?" Joshua's heart thundered.

"She was taken to a local boarding house."

"A boarding house?"

Kenan frowned and Joshua shuddered at the darkness that passed over his features. "It's a cathouse run by a soiled dove named Mrs. Appleby."

"What in the hell is Rosie doin' going to a cathouse?"

"If it was Rosie."

"Where is this place?"

"Just along the main street. Small, he said, built onto another building."

"Well, let's check it out."

"Joshua…"

"Yeah."

"Try to stay calm. I know how hard it is. I'm mad as a hornet at the thought of what could've happened, but I've been in a similar situation before and it helps to keep a cool head."

"Sure." Joshua lifted his hat and pushed his hair back from his forehead then settled his Stetson back into place. He'd keep a cool head as long as that calico queen hadn't allowed any harm to come to his Rosie.

* * * *

Rosie stuffed her belongings back into her bag then reached beneath the mattress. She pulled out the parcel containing Kenan's money and tucked it back under her corset. She tried not to touch her stomach, not wanting to acknowledge the decision she had made earlier that day. It was something she would deal with later. Right now, all she wanted was to go home. But she knew that she would need to wait until morning. There was a stage due into Nevada City early the next day and she intended to be on it. But for now, she was ready.

The house was still quiet. Mrs. Appleby and the other women had not yet surfaced, but Rosie felt sure that they would do soon. They would, no doubt, be hungry. She decided to head down to the kitchen to make them a farewell meal. Though not companions she would choose to reside with, the women had been understanding and tolerant of her, if not all as kind as Mrs. Appleby. But then, their lives were not as happy as Rosie's had been. And she could see that now. She had always loved her life, adored being surrounded by her brothers then by Catherine and the baby, but falling in love with Joshua had somehow unsettled that, as if reminding her of what she might be missing. It had made her long for something that she hadn't previously wanted or even needed. But that side of her life was over, she had confirmed that when she had risen at noon, and now she was ready to embrace her life back at the Duggan homestead.

Whatever it might bring.

She padded quietly down the stairs and headed through the small front parlor and into the kitchen area. The fire had gone out so she set about lighting it then made coffee and started to prepare supper. The simple act brought memories of all the times she had made supper for her family rushing back and she smiled, her heart lifted by the thought that soon she would be home again. She wouldn't die alone in a strange place. She wouldn't leave her family wondering what had happened to her, suffering that terrible fate of never knowing where she was or if she had needed them.

Just then, a sound came from the front of the house. A tapping. There was someone at the door.

What should she do? She could answer it, but it might be a gentleman caller seeking out one of Mrs. Appleby's young women. What if he mistook her for one of them? She shuddered. How awful to be in a position where you had to sell your body to a stranger, to allow a man to do those things that she had done with Joshua. She loved Joshua and had wanted his kisses, his caresses, and to feel him inside her, but to have a man you didn't love touching you so intimately... It was more repugnant than she could articulate.

The knocking came again. This time louder and more insistent. Whoever was out there, had no intention of going away. She had better deal with them before they woke the whole household.

She made her way to the front door and opened it a crack, then gasped as she saw a familiar face.

"Excuse me, ma'am..."

Rosie opened the door wide and looked down at the man who had brought her to Mrs. Appleby's following her arrival in Nevada City.

"Yes?"

"I thought you'd like to know that there are two men in town asking after ya."

"Two men?" Rosie's stomach lurched. Who was it likely to be? Kenan and one of her other brothers, probably.

"Yeah...a real tall dark-haired one and another with fairer hair. I was over at the General store when the dark-haired one came in. Ya know, now I think about it, he actually looked a bit like you. But a bigger, male version, of course." He laughed as if amused at his own comment. "Store owner told 'em he thought you'd come here. So I'm giving you fair warning." He eyed her as if suspecting her of being guilty of some crime that led her to be pursued. It made goosebumps rise on her skin, and she shivered as if someone had just stepped on her grave.

"Oh. Thank you. That's...um...very kind." Rosie made to close the door but he continued to stand there. He wanted money. "Hold on."

She closed the door and slid a hand beneath her corset. She pulled out the parcel and quickly removed a coin before returning the rest of the money to its hiding place. When she opened the door again to hand over the money, the man's face was ashen and he gestured over his shoulder. "Too late. Sorry!" He held out his hand and Rosie dropped the coin into it and watched as he lumbered off the porch and out into the street.

Then she met the dark eyes of her twin brother.

"Rosie." He hurried forward and grabbed her upper arms. "You're safe and well?" The emotion in his face broke her heart and she fell gratefully against his chest. "Oh, Rosie, you had us all so worried."

When she had caught her breath, Rosie gazed at him again. "Kenan, I feel like I've been away for years. It's so good to see you. I've never been so relieved to see anyone in all my days."

"Not even me?" The voice that came from behind Kenan startled Rosie and she gasped. She peered around her brother's broad shoulders to meet Joshua's intense blue eyes.

"Joshua. I…what…I mean…"

"We've come to take you home, Rosie." Joshua appeared ten years older than when she'd last seen him.

Rosie moved out of Kenan's embrace and took Joshua's proffered hand. How would he feel about the decision she had made earlier that day? A decision that affected him as much as it did her. Could she tell him? Her heart sank. Not yet. There was no need to blight the moment with that information. It would wait.

"Will you come home with us, Rosie?"

"Yes. Take me home. Please."

* * * *

They traveled home with Rosie riding behind Joshua. Kenan had said that she should ride with him on his mare because she was an unmarried woman and it would not be proper for her to ride with Joshua.

Rosie sensed that there was something they weren't telling her. The two men had had several whispered conversations when they stopped to rest the horses, and she ached to know what they discussed.

She was acutely aware of Joshua watching her constantly, as if he was afraid that she would disappear again. It was as if he needed to keep looking at her to believe that she was safe. It made her warm with delight. He really cared for her.

They set up a temporary camp at the riverside and Kenan wandered off to find firewood, leaving her and Joshua briefly alone.

"Rosie...I was so worried about you." Joshua took her hands and kissed them. Rosie jumped at his touch, her eager flesh shocked into life at his proximity. She had been away just days yet missed him as she would a part of herself. It was different to the way that she missed him when he was out on the cattle trail. She knew then that he would return to her and she counted the days until she could hold him again. But this time *she* had been the one away from home, and she had felt his absence from her embrace all the more intensely. The pain had actually been physical and she had been stunned by its palpable essence. Was this what real love was like then?

"I am sorry for that, Joshua. I just didn't know what else to do."

Joshua stared into her eyes. "Rosie, I love you with everything that I am. You have to know this. When we get back, I have matters to deal with, but I promise you that I will not be long away from you. I will join you at your home as soon as I can. But please promise me that you will wait for me. Do not disappear again, because I could not bear it."

Rosie's heart cracked at the anxiety in his expression and she wished that she could take back the past few days and make him feel safe and secure once more.

"I promise," she said, wishing that she was free from the burden she now carried in her heart, the secret knowledge of her difficult decision. If only they could move forward together. But it would not be possible until Joshua knew the truth.

Kenan carried a pile of wood over to them and began to build a fire, and Rosie knew that her confession would have to wait until they were home.

* * * *

Rosie lifted herself on the saddle and peered over Kenan's shoulder at a sight that made her throat ache and her heart thunder.

Home.

She had thanked Mrs. Appleby for her kindness before leaving Nevada City and Kenan had insisted on paying her extra for the time of Rosie's stay. However, as helpful as Mrs. Appleby had been, Rosie had been desperate to return to the Duggan homestead.

She was back where she belonged. Though she had been gone just days, it felt like far longer, and she couldn't wait to settle back in.

Joshua had left them at the outskirts of Virginia City, repeating his promises from the night before.

He won't be long. He'll join us soon. She played the words over and over in her head to reassure her fluttering heart.

But, of course, when he did arrive and they had the opportunity to talk properly…then she would have to tell him. *Everything.* And that thought sent ice through her veins.

"What is it Rosie? You just shuddered like someone walked over your grave." Kenan turned in the saddle. "I thought you'd be glad to be home."

"Oh I am, Kenan. I am *so* happy to be back. I just felt a little cold."

"Well, we'll get you inside and Catherine will no doubt have coffee on. Then we'll get the tub filled so as you can bathe."

"Why, brother, do I smell?"

"I didn't wanna say anything…" She felt Kenan's broad shoulders shake with laughter. "But you do smell a bit strange."

She poked him in the ribs and laughed with him in spite of her anxiety. Being in a different house, sleeping in a different bed then riding for hours on horseback could well affect how she smelled. She realized that she probably was stale and dusty.

Besides, a bath would be welcome to ease her aching limbs, and hopefully it would release some of the tension she carried in her shoulders, even if it would not wash away the fear she carried in her heart.

* * * *

Joshua turned to the man at his side.

"Come on, sir, we have a place to be!"

The preacher smiled as he dug his heels into his fat mare. "I know, Mr. Hampton. You're keen to get wed."

"Indeed, sir. I have waited long enough…too long, in fact, to do this."

As his horse covered the grassy plains, his stomach churned with a mixture of excitement and nerves. He had one more thing to do before he could make his way to the Duggan homestead, and he was not looking forward to it at all. He could have gone to the Hampton ranch first then headed into town but he'd feared being unable to locate a preacher, so he'd wanted to secure one before he made his announcement to his family.

"Right, I'm gonna have a quick word with my father then we'll be on our way. You happy to wait here?"

The preacher nodded his gray head at Joshua. "I'll wait here, sir. The good Lord gifted me with patience, indeed."

Joshua stared at him for a moment. He had near enough kidnapped the religious man, pulled him away from his breakfast and forced him to saddle his horse. But he had explained his urgency and reassured the preacher that he would be handsomely recompensed for his time. Money was a powerful tool in the art of persuasion.

"I'm not going anywhere, Mr. Hampton." The preacher smiled. "You have my word as a man of God."

That would have to be enough then.

Joshua climbed the porch steps and took a steadying breath before opening the door. Time to do it. Time to be a man.

The living room was empty so he strode through into the large kitchen. His mother stood at the table kneading dough and his father sat at the far end, away from the flour, making notes in his ledger. They looked at Joshua as he approached.

"So you've returned." Dylan Hampton stated the obvious. "Alone, I'm pleased to see. Would you like to explain exactly why you rushed off three days ago with Kenan Duggan...without a word to me or your mother? We had to hear it from your brothers, Joshua. That's not exactly showing your folks respect we deserve, is it?"

"Never mind that. I didn't have time to speak to you before I left. I've come to tell you something." Joshua was surprised at his own firm tone.

Dylan Hampton glanced at his wife then closed his ledger. "Take a seat, Joshua."

"I've no time for that." Joshua gritted his teeth. He scanned his father's pale face, willing the older man to be strong but understanding. If there was ever a time when Joshua needed his pa to listen, to really listen and to accept what he heard, then this was it.

"What's the hurry, Joshua?" His mother smiled but her eyes were wary. She eyed his face then stared at her husband as if assessing who was most likely to be the victor in this clashing of horns.

"I have something to tell you, Pa. You won't like it but…my mind's made up."

"Joshua, son." His father frowned as he stood and placed a trembling hand on Joshua's shoulder. "You don't have to do this. Really…"

"Really I do, Pa."

"Joshua—" Mrs. Hampton's face was flushed and she dusted her hands on her apron. "Don't throw everything away."

"I'm not, Ma. I'm grabbing my life by the reins and taking control now. As Pa said I should do. I'm heading over to the Duggan homestead and there…this afternoon…I'm gonna make Rosie Duggan my wife." There. It was out. There was no retreat.

"You will not." His mother gasped, her mouth opening and closing.

Joshua inclined his head. "Indeed I will. I didn't have to let you know. But I wanted to. I owe you that as my parents. I respect you and love you. I always have. But this is something I have to do. You can come with me and help me and my bride to celebrate, or…" He shrugged. He held his breath. He swallowed hard.

Mrs. Hampton sank onto a bench and shook her head. Joshua's father watched her before turning back to him. "This is a mistake, Joshua. An enormous mistake. If you do this then you're cutting yourself out of everything I've worked for. The possibilities here. Look at what you've done to your mother. How can you do this to her, to me… How can you throw all this away?" He gestured at the room and at the landscape beyond the windows.

"I love Rosie, Pa. Love her like I've never loved anyone or anything. Whatever chances we take by being together are worth taking. Being without her, for the rest of my life, and knowing that I abandoned her when we had the chance to be together – that's not the road I want to follow. So you can keep your ranch. I know you built it from scratch and I congratulate you on that. I have never said anything different. You've done well for yourself and I respect you for it. Ma?"

His mother glanced at him.

"I love you, too, and respect how you brought all of us Hampton kids up. But there comes a time in a man's life when he has to move on, to carve out his own way. You did it, Pa. Now it's my time. I've chosen my wife. You can accept my choice or not. But just as you've told me that I have no place here if I wed her, then I'm telling you, if you refuse to accept Rosie, then you've no place in our lives either." Emotion welled in his chest, threatening to burst forth in a torrent of angry words, but he swallowed it. He would not create a scene. He would not upset his folks more than he had to. He did love and respect them, but that love and respect had to be a two-way thing.

He patted his father's shoulder then squeezed his mother's as he passed. She tensed beneath his fingers. He had displeased her mightily. His pa, too. But he had done the right thing.

"We'll marry this afternoon at two. You are welcome if you change your minds."

He picked up his hat then walked out of the room without looking back.

"Come on then, preacher." Joshua nodded at the man who still sat in his saddle, sweating as the day warmed up.

"Yes, sir" — the man saluted — "let's go meet your bride."

Joshua mounted his horse then turned her and spurred her onward, toward the home Kenan had told him to call his own and toward the woman he wanted at his side for the rest of his life.

Chapter Eleven

Rosie sat on the edge of her bed and stared blankly into the corner of the room. A cobweb fluttered in the draft that stole through the wooden boards but she barely registered its presence. Catherine combed through Rosie's damp hair and her gentle touch made Rosie sleepy.

"Nearly done," Catherine said.

"Do you know what's going on, Catherine?"

"Whatever do you mean, dear?"

Rosie heard the smile in Catherine's voice.

"You do," Rosie accused. "Making me bathe and wash my hair then suggesting I put on my best gown."

"Oh, come on, Rosie," Catherine walked around and sat on the bed next to her. She dried the comb on her apron. "You must have your suspicions."

"I do." Rosie nodded. "But I'm afraid to hope in case I'm wrong. Am I…getting married?"

"Yes! This afternoon. And it's about time."

Rosie stared at the dress that hung from the peg on the back of the door. So Joshua wanted to marry her.

They would marry.

Today.

Her heart leaped.

Then it sank.

"What is it, Rosie? Aren't you happy?" Catherine scanned her face and Rosie flushed.

"It's not that."

"Then what?"

"I..." How could she explain what had happened in Nevada City? Her visit to the midwife. Would Catherine understand?

"Rosie, you are my sister and I love you. You can tell me."

Just then, there was a murmur from the cradle at the foot of the bed. Catherine, a devoted mother, took the baby everywhere. She got to her feet and went to her child. "Shhh, little one."

Little one.

Rosie felt the walls closing in on her, their wooden panels crushing her and squeezing her tightly, and she gasped for breath.

"What is it? Did I fasten your corset too tightly?" Catherine hurried to Rosie's side and began to loosen her stays.

Rosie shook her head. "No...it's not that. I have something, something awful that I need to tell Joshua. I must tell him but I fear it will turn him against me. That it will alter how he...how he sees me."

She tasted the salt of her tears as they ran down her face.

"Oh, Rosie, it cannot be that bad."

"It is." Rosie rubbed at her eyes. "It is."

"Then you must be honest with him, Rosie." Catherine cupped Rosie's cheeks in her cool hands. "You should not have secrets between you before you marry. I had to be honest with Kenan before we wed. It was an incredibly difficult thing to do and I did not know if it would make him turn from me in disgust but I could not live a lie."

"And he understood?" Rosie watched as Catherine ran a finger over the scars on the inside of her right arm.

"Yes. He was wonderful...because he loved me. And I'm sure that Joshua will be, too."

"Yes. I'm sure he will be." Rosie clenched her hands together in her lap. *At least I hope he will be. But even if he understands, will he ever be able to forgive me?*

"Now, let us finish getting you ready." Catherine removed the gown from its peg and brought it to Rosie. She stood dutifully and allowed her sister-in-law to dress her, making her ready for the wedding that might well not happen once Joshua heard what she had to say.

* * * *

Joshua paced the porch. His stomach grumbled and he placed a hand over it as if to silence it. He hadn't eaten since early that morning and he didn't think he'd be able to force anything down for a while. He was taut with nerves but also excitement. If Rosie was happy to become his wife, then he would soon be a married man.

He glanced across the yard and the surrounding fields then beyond that toward the golden haze of the horizon. Would his folks come? He doubted it very much. They'd seemed set on their decision. And he was set on his. He would marry the woman he loved above all else, and do all he could to make her happy. To give her a good life as she deserved.

The door to the homestead swung open and he held his breath, expecting Rosie, but it was Catherine.

"Hi, Joshua. You clean up well." A smile played across Catherine's lips but Joshua was too agitated to return it.

"Is she coming?"

"Yes, Joshua. She'll be out in a moment. But..."

Joshua felt cold hands tighten around his neck. *But...*

"She said she'd like to speak with you first. Alone."

"Sure. I'll wait here." He pointed at the porch then flushed at how ridiculous his statement was. Of course he'd wait there. Where else would he be?

Kenan and his brothers walked past from the barn, carrying planks of wood and a small trestle table. They began to place them in a line at the side of the house with the table at the far end. They were creating an aisle, Joshua realized, for Rosie to walk along. The cold hands squeezed, making it hard to swallow. What did she want to speak to him about? Would she refuse to go through with this?

"Joshua." He turned to see a vision of beauty that stole his breath away.

He gasped then sucked in air. "Rosie."

She wore her long, dark hair down and it shone like black satin as it fell over her shoulders. Her dress was the same color as her warm amber eyes and it seemed to reflect on her pale skin, giving it a golden glow, a luminescence which made her appear almost ethereal. Joshua shivered. In that moment he knew in his bones that if he couldn't have this woman as his wife, he would never love another. *Ever*. Rosie was the only woman for him.

"We need to talk, my love." Rosie reached for his hand.

"We do?"

"Please. Can we walk?"

He took her hand in the crook of his arm and they walked off the stoop and across the yard. He placed his free hand over Rosie's and stroked gently, savoring the warmth of her skin, the strength of the sinews beneath. Rosie was no upper-class woman, she worked at the homestead, keeping it running alongside her brothers. But he loved her even more for the signs that would tell any stranger this. She had no airs and graces and there was no pretense about her. She would be a good wife and a wonderful mother, if they were lucky enough to make a child together.

When they had passed through the gate of the perimeter fence, he led Rosie to the shelter of an old tree and they stood in the cool shadows beneath its foliage, facing the homestead. He waited, though the silence was agony.

"Joshua..." Rosie ran her eyes over his face and he felt them there as he would feel her touch. His heartbeat quickened and he licked his lips. Even now, he longed to pull her to his chest and shower her face with kisses.

"Rosie?"

"I have something I need to tell you and I'm...I'm afraid to in case it alters how you see me but also I need to...because I would be honest with you always."

"Nothing you could say would change how I feel about you, sweetheart." He stroked her cheeks, rubbing his thumbs over her lips, then he leaned forward and kissed her. Gently. Her fragrance washed over him, sweet and uplifting as honeysuckle, fresh and mouth-watering as apples. He moved in for another kiss but she placed her hand over his lips.

"No. Please. You'll distract me, and I must say this first or I'll lose my nerve."

"Then lose your nerve, Rosie. I don't care about anything as long as you love me. I want you as my wife. Let's get married and we can talk later." Fear throbbed in Joshua's gut, cold and heavy. He would prefer not to know anything that could alter the course he had chosen. He was exhausted by change, by insecurity, and by the fear that someone would step in and take away the chance he had for happiness with Rosie. He did not want anything, whatever it was, to prevent him taking her to wife.

"Joshua, I must tell you. I will not enter into a marriage when there are things unsaid. I will not." She shook her head and he watched as her hair swept across her breasts, revealing the tops of the plump mounds, which showed at her neckline. He fought the urge to place a hand there, where amber satin met rose hued skin, so that he could touch her, possess her, caress her in the way he knew she loved. More than ever, she was softer, rounder, more feminine.

"Then speak, for I cannot wait much longer to make you mine for eternity." He smiled, hoping to relax her, but she bit her lip instead and lowered her eyes.

"Joshua, I love you. With everything that I am, I love you. For a time, I was afraid that you did not feel the same..."

"No! How could I not have? I adore you, Rosie. I am so sorry that I did not sort things out sooner."

"That is of no consequence now, my love. I know and understand. But when I left and went away I did something bad."

"Rosie, how could you have done something bad? You are too good, too sweet to hurt anyone or anything." His heartbeat increased and his blood rushed hot and noisy in his ears.

"Oh, Joshua, that is not true."

Rosie covered her mouth with trembling hands and gasped repeatedly. Joshua watched as her eyes brimmed with tears that trickled down her cheeks and over her fingers. What could she have done?

"Come now," he pulled her into his arms and kissed the top of her head, "tell me and let us become husband and wife."

Rosie pulled away from Joshua's comfort then glanced at his face and took a deep breath. How to explain? How could she tell him exactly what had happened to her when she was away and when she thought that they could never be joined in matrimony?

She shivered. Though the day was warm, she was chilled to the bone.

Joshua reached for her but she avoided the comfort of his touch. "No, Joshua. Let me speak then you can decide if you still want me in your life."

Her stomach churned and her throat ached. She longed to forget, to move on, to push her sins from her mind and become Mrs. Joshua Hampton, but she had to do this first.

"When I went away, I thought it was for the best. I believed that I could set you free from any obligation and that I was doing the right thing."

"Oh, Rosie, did you think that I wouldn't come after you?"

She shook her head. "I had hoped...I guess I knew... Oh, what's the use? I did what I hoped was the right thing."

"But of course it wasn't, sweetheart. I love you and I need you by my side."

Oh please repeat that in five minutes' time.

"I hadn't been feeling well for a while but I attributed it to heartache at knowing that I should leave you. Only, when I was away I discovered that I was, in fact, with child." Rosie worried her lower lip and stared hard at the ground. She fixed her eyes onto a tiny bug that gripped a blade of grass and watched as it held on in spite of the persistence of the breeze. She felt like that bug, hanging on for dear life, afraid that she would be unsettled any moment.

"You are with child?" Joshua grabbed her hands and pulled her close. "Oh, Rosie, that is such good news. I am to be a father." He cradled her to his chest and Rosie's vision blurred.

"Wait, Joshua. Please. Wait."

He released her gently then tipped her chin up. "What is it?"

"The woman, Mrs. Appleby, who I lodged with, suggested that if I was to be alone then I might not want..." Her throat closed over. "I might not want to...to keep the child."

Joshua scanned her face. His eyes were blank for a moment then, as realization dawned, they filled with what Rosie could only describe as terror. He opened and closed his mouth as if searching for words he was unable to find.

Rosie placed a trembling hand on his chest and smoothed it over his shirt front.

"Joshua... She took me to a midwife...a local woman who examined me and confirmed that I was indeed expecting a babe. She gave me a paste, an herbal concoction, which she told me to consume. But only, and she stressed this, only if I would wake the following morning to find myself bleeding." The words seemed to fill her mouth with the salty tang of blood, and bile rose in her throat.

Joshua pushed his hands through his hair and turned to gaze out across the plains. His jaw twitched and his Adam's apple bobbed.

"Joshua? Tell me what you're thinking, please. I cannot bear it."

He paused and swallowed before turning back to face her. "So there is no child."

"No, Joshua, no."

"Oh, Rosie, I am so sorry, I—"

"No, my love, what I mean is that I returned to my lodgings with the paste and spent the afternoon in thought. I remembered in vivid detail every kiss we had shared, all the plans we had made, and most of all how much I love you. How completely you lift my heart when you smile and how much I adore holding you to my breast. How much..." A sob strangled her words. "Joshua, I could not do it. I resolved to find a way to keep the babe, to make a life for us, even if I could not be your wife, and even if you would not be able to care for us."

Joshua eyed her stomach. When she placed a hand there, he covered it with his own, and she was immediately reassured by the warmth of his touch.

"You need worry no longer, Rosie. I will provide for you both."

"But can you ever forgive me?"

"Forgive you? But what for?"

"I thought, if just for the briefest time, of destroying our child. Surely that is unforgiveable?"

Joshua smiled as he ran a finger over her cheek then settled his hand on her shoulder. "Rosie, whatever you thought, you did not do it, and I am convinced that you never would have. You are a good woman, and I know how much you adore children. You would never have killed our baby...whatever you thought lay ahead of you."

Rosie's heart thundered and she focused on slowing her breathing. It would not be good for the little one if she became distressed. And now, all would be well, for Joshua Hampton didn't hate her. He understood why she had considered doing the unthinkable. Why she had *not* done it. That she never would have done it. For he knew her and loved her and she could ask for no more.

"Now, I have one more question for you, Rosie."

She steeled herself, preparing for whatever it might be.

"Will you marry me today and be mine for the rest of your days?"

She smiled and took his hands, moving into his warm embrace.

"Yes, Joshua Hampton. I am ready to become your wife."

Joshua's eyes changed then, and Rosie sighed as she registered the desire within them. He took hold of her shoulders and moved her gently around the tree so that it obscured them from the house, then he kissed her with a warmth and passion that made her heart swell and her body tingle.

Rosie leaned against the thick, hard trunk, allowing it to support her as Joshua ran his large hands down her sides then up over her stomach to cup her breasts through the soft fabric. Her nipples pebbled beneath his familiar fingers and heat rushed through her body.

"Joshua...we can't...not here!"

Please, here. Now.

"I can't wait until later, Rosie. I need you so badly."

Rosie glanced around the tree and was glad to see that her brothers were still busy arranging the yard. "We might have a little time."

"Yes." He lowered his head and kissed the tops of her breasts until she moaned with the heady need that flowed through her veins. Her body was so responsive, so sensitive, and she longed to feel Joshua's hands all over her as he buried himself deep inside her.

Suddenly wanton, she lifted her skirts and slid down her bloomers then grinned as he loosened his trousers. The bulge beneath his belt informed her that he was ready to make love to her.

"This is...naughty, Joshua. A little wanton, don't you think?"

"It will be our final time before we marry, Rosie. I think we can indulge ourselves." He raised his eyebrows and Rosie giggled in response. They were to be married. They would have a child. Everything would be just fine and dandy.

Joshua freed his length and Rosie whimpered at the jolt of desire that curled in her sex. She wanted this man. To be joined both physically and emotionally with him.

He took her thighs in his hands and lifted her so that her legs rested around his waist then he slid slowly inside her. Rosie rested her head on his chest and allowed the gentle rocking of their bodies to carry her along the pleasure wave. The summer breeze toyed with her hair, Joshua's strength held her in place and their bodies met as they joined in the instinctive pursuit of ecstasy.

In mere moments, Rosie felt the hot rush of intense ripples as they spread from her core and exploded in all the parts of her that made her a woman. Then

Joshua increased his pace and soon swelled inside her before filling her with his heat and covering her mouth with his own.

"My wife," he whispered when he pulled away from their kiss.

"Always," Rosie replied as she met his satisfied gaze.

Chapter Twelve

Rosie stood on the porch and looked out at the yard. Her brothers had done a good job of creating an aisle out of the benches taken from the house, which Catherine had hastily adorned with a variety of wild flowers plucked fresh from the prairie. A gentle breeze cooled the warm afternoon and carried with it the scents of summer, of home and of hope.

"Are you ready, sister?"

Rosie met Kenan's warm brown eyes and smiled. Her lips twitched as she did so, betraying her nerves and high emotions.

"Yes, brother. I am ready."

Kenan held out his arm and Rosie took it. Her stomach fluttered so she placed her free hand over it gently. *Yes, little one, time to create our family.* She frowned as she cupped the slight bump. Had it been the child moving then and not just her anxiety like butterflies within? *No, it's too soon.* But the thought that there was a chance, however small, that she had just felt her baby quicken within her womb brought tears to her eyes. She would be a wife and a mother.

The two things she had longed for yet never really believed she would gain.

Suddenly, a sweet tune began inside the homestead. It seemed to come from deep within, quiet and calm but then increasing in strength. It grew and grew, getting louder by the second, until Emmett appeared in the doorway. He flashed Rosie a grin before deftly stepping past her, the small Irish fiddle tucked under his chin as he played an old, haunting and familiar tune.

It proved too much, hearing a song that her father used to play, and Rosie gave in to the torrent of emotion as the tears coursed down her cheeks and sobs wracked her chest.

She blinked as Joshua appeared at her side and pulled her into his strong embrace then held there until her shaking ceased.

"Rosie...sweetheart. Emmett did not mean to upset you so. He thought only to play a tune that would remind you of your father and happy memories."

Rosie sniffed and patted a handkerchief Joshua had placed in her hand to her eyes.

"Oh my darling, I am just extremely happy and I think that" – she lowered her voice – "the pregnancy is making me more emotional."

"I know." He kissed her cheeks, her forehead, her lips. "And I am happy, too. But I'm also keen to get through the day so that I can hold you in my arms and snuggle you in my bed as my wife." He pressed his lips to her ear. "The tree on the prairie was wonderful but not as comfortable as a bed will be."

Rosie's cheeks warmed and she glanced around them, but her siblings, sister-in-law and the preacher were standing a respectable distance away.

"Shall we try again?" Joshua asked.

"Yes. Let's." Rosie nodded.

Joshua made his way over to the preacher, where he stood grinning back at her.

Rosie held a hand out to Kenan. He took his position at her side again and Emmett began a new tune, then Rosie began the happiest walk of her life.

When they had reached the end of the aisle, Kenan kissed Rosie's cheek then gave her hand to Joshua. Kenan stared at Rosie for a moment, his eyes like burning coals, and she realized that he was filled with a mixture of happiness and nostalgia. As twins, they had always been close, and for a long time he had been the main man in her life, but now he was giving that position to another. As it should be. But for a man like Kenan, handing over responsibility was tough and he would worry, no doubt, about whether Joshua was up to the task.

Rosie, however, had no qualms at all.

Joshua squeezed her fingers and she felt that he was trembling. He shifted from one foot to the other as if standing barefoot on hot sand. *He's nervous, poor love. In spite of his reassurances, he is anxious, too.* Rosie leaned forward and whispered into his ear, "All will be well, my love. This is as it should be."

Joshua's eyes lit up and he kissed her quickly, causing her to giggle.

"Now, now, Mr. Hampton, there will be time enough for that later," the preacher scolded.

"Yes, sir." Joshua nodded. He removed his Stetson and placed it on a nearby bench.

The music slowed then ceased and Emmett came to stand at Kenan's side. Rosie glanced around her. Kenan stood with his arm around Catherine and she rocked gently, nursing the babe to her chest. Matthew was grinning as if he'd just won a hand of poker and was about to collect his winnings. Emmett still held the fiddle and bow in his hands as he waited for the preacher to begin. And Joshua was at her side, tall, handsome, muscular. A man. *Her* man. Soon to be her husband.

It was perfect and she vowed to treasure this moment forever so that she could relate it to her children and one day her grandchildren in vivid detail.

"Let us begin." The preacher opened a small, battered bible and started to read a sermon. Rosie listened to the familiar words and tried to focus her eyes on the religious man, but Joshua's presence ignited her senses and sent a warm glow throughout her body.

"And do you, Rosie Duggan, swear to take this man—"

"What's that?" Joshua raised a hand to shade his eyes as he peered into the distance. A cloud of dust swirled around, obscuring their view, but Rosie could hear the far off hoofbeats of several horses. Her chest tightened and a chill crept over her despite the warmth of the day. It had all been too good to be true. She should have known it.

She had come so close to becoming Joshua's wife, but now someone or something was about to put a stop to her dreams.

Joshua wrapped an arm around Rosie's shoulders and pulled her close as it became clear who rode toward the homestead.

"Your family," Rosie whispered, resting her head against his chest.

"What in the hell are they doin' here?" Joshua growled as he squeezed Rosie even tighter.

Her heart thumped, and she longed to scream with the unfairness of it all. Why were they coming to her home? Today of all days.

But she knew. All too well. They came to stop her wedding. To crush her dreams. To steal away her happiness.

"Are they here to cause trouble?" Kenan stood at Joshua's side and frowned at the approaching crowd.

Joshua shrugged. "I...I guess so... I told them we were getting wed, but I didn't think they'd come, so I guess it's trouble they're after."

Kenan turned to Catherine. "Take Rosie and the little one into the house. Stay there." He glanced at Rosie then back at his wife. Catherine nodded.

"No, Kenan. I want to know why they've come. I'll not hide away inside."

"Rosie—" Joshua pressed his lips to her forehead and cupped her face in his warm hands. "Go inside. Please. It might not be pretty, and I've no desire to see you upset on our wedding day."

"Joshua, I can't. I'm sorry but I need to know the truth. I *need* to hear it. There's no sense in hiding from it."

He paused for a moment and Rosie trembled as she held his gaze. She willed him to be strong and to do the right thing. To do what he needed to do, not what he thought was best for everyone else.

"You're right, sweetheart. It should all be out in the open now. But whatever they say, you remember that I love you and that we're" —he offered a shy smile— "we're almost wed."

Rosie tried to return the smile but her lips refused to cooperate. They remained tight and pained, locked in a grimace of anxiety as her lover's relatives reached the perimeter fence.

"Afternoon!" Dylan Hampton dismounted and tethered his horse to the fence then walked the remaining distance to stand before his son. He was followed by two of his sons and, Rosie lowered her eyes to hide her surprise, by his wife.

"What are you doin' here?" Joshua moved forward so that he half-obscured Rosie from his father.

"Now, son, that's no way to greet your pa."

"I asked what you're doin' here. If you've come to try to stir up a hornet's nest then you can just turn right around and get back on your horses. You too, Ma."

Rosie placed a steadying hand on Joshua's shoulder. He was strong and muscular beneath her hand, and taut as a wildcat ready to spring. She felt the sinews of his flesh as they tensed and she realized that Mr. Hampton was likely to catch a tongue-lashing if nothing else.

Dylan Hampton removed his hat and ran a hand through his sweat-dampened hair. His scalp was visible through the gray and Rosie saw him for the first time as an aging man. Not as a rancher to fear, but as a man in his fifties. His face was haggard, as if he had lost weight suddenly, and his eyes were dull. In fact, if she wasn't mistaken, he bore the appearance of one suffering from an ailment. She had been right about him when he'd come to the homestead the day of Catherine's labor. Her chest tightened. Was Mr. Hampton ill? And if so, was Joshua aware? He had said nothing of it to her.

"Joshua, we've not come for trouble. Just to ask if you're certain that this is the right thing to do."

Mrs. Hampton tucked her arm into her husband's and Rosie watched the tender way that she held on to him. As if afraid to hold him too tightly in case she hurt him, yet also nervous about letting go in case she lost him.

"Joshua, please don't be mad. We thought only for the best. It's all we've ever wanted for you and your siblings. The best..." She looked at Rosie. "And if this young woman is the one who makes you happy, then we've no quarrel with your choice."

Joshua turned to Rosie and she registered the confusion on his face. He had not expected this, not at all, and he had still intended to marry her — in spite of his parents' feelings. Yet here they were, dust covered and saddle weary, having ridden over to the homestead in the afternoon heat, to tell their son that they would accept his choice. Blood rushed through Rosie's ears and into her cheeks and she stumbled forward.

Before she reached her knees, Joshua scooped her up and pressed her against his chest.

"Rosie, my love, are you well?"

She nodded. "Yes. I just felt a little warm."

"The baby?" he whispered into her ear.

"Is well, I am sure."

"Can we continue?"

"Yes. Please."

He placed her gently onto her feet then gestured at the benches. "Well, you're welcome to stay if you'd like, but I'll have no more interruptions. I'm about to make Rosie Duggan my wife."

The Hamptons appeared relieved at Joshua's certainty. There was no arguing with a man who was that self-assured and in command of his own life. They sat on the benches and Joshua took Rosie's hand as the preacher resumed the ceremony and Rosie finally married the man she loved.

* * * *

Rosie leaned against Joshua's chest, listening to his strong heartbeat and steady, deep breaths. The gray light of dawn seeped into their bedroom and she savored the cool of the early morning, knowing that soon the August heat would become near unbearable. It had been two months since their wedding and she was now five months into her pregnancy.

A flutter in her stomach brought a smile to her face and she rolled onto her back and placed a hand over the bump. Beneath her touch, a foot or a hand pressed upward and she stifled a giggle, afraid of waking her husband.

She had never thought to be so happy, so fulfilled and so contented. She had everything she could ever have wished for and life was so much more than she had thought it could be. Occasionally, fear sneaked in beneath the door and worried her, whispering about things that could go wrong, but Rosie always banished it quickly and tried to reassure herself by thinking of the happy times her family had shared of late and of the joy that the babe in her belly would bring.

She was gently roused by a delicious sensation as Joshua ran his hands over her body. She opened her eyes to find him kneeling next to her, the blankets pushed to the bottom of the bed. They were both naked but the room was warm.

She smiled as Joshua stroked over her shoulders then cupped her full breasts. As her pregnancy had progressed, her curves had grown, and her husband delighted in the fullness of her figure, which made her feel beautiful. Joshua caressed her all the way down to the tips of her toes then back up again, deliberately avoiding her ebony curls, until she stilled his hands.

"You tease me, my love."

"Me?" He raised his eyebrows. "What would you like me to do?"

Rosie sighed. "As if you don't know by now."

He saluted her then straddled her body and kissed a trail over the chocolate brown peaks of her nipples and down to her thighs. He parted them and positioned himself between them then leaned forward and kissed her mound. Rosie whimpered as he parted her with his thumbs then flicked his tongue over her bud until it swelled. He teased her opening with a fingertip, circling her needy flesh yet not thrusting inside her as she yearned for him to do.

"I need you," she whispered.

"Whatever my wife wants," he replied.

He moved over her then rolled her gently onto her side and spooned her. Rosie pressed against him and he slipped into her easily, gripping her hips with his strong hands.

As they moved together, Joshua cupped her breasts and squeezed her nipples until they were tight peaks, then he took Rosie's hand and placed it over her folds so she could feel where they were joined. He held her hand there and it rubbed against her bud as he thrust deeper, bringing her to satisfying, shuddering fulfilment, closely followed by his own.

They stayed as they were then, still joined and as close as they could be, and Rosie allowed herself to drift into a sweet, sated sleep.

* * * *

A loud noise from outside jerked Rosie back to full consciousness.

"Joshua!" She shook her husband.

He opened his eyes and smiled at her, wrapping an arm around her waist and pulling her toward him.

"No, my love," she smiled in spite of herself, "there's something going on outside."

Joshua frowned and sat up then reached for his clothes. Rosie admired his broad shoulders and the shapely curve of his behind as he stood and stepped into his trousers then pulled on his shirt.

"Stay here," he warned, a frown creasing his handsome face. "I'll find out what's going on."

Rosie flung her legs over the edge of the bed. *Stay here? Not likely.* She pulled her shift over her head and followed it with her housedress then she hurried into the main room of the homestead.

Kenan stood in the doorway with Joshua peering over his shoulder. There was someone outside, speaking in urgent, hushed tones. She edged closer, keen to hear what was being said, but the interloper was clearly agitated and his words were garbled.

Joshua turned and caught her watching them.

"What is it?" Rosie approached him and placed her hands on his chest.

"Yes, what's wrong?" Catherine crossed the room to Rosie's side, her chubby cheeked child balanced on her hip.

Joshua frowned. "I think Kenan had better speak to you about this, Catherine."

Rosie wrapped an arm around Catherine's shoulder as her sister-in-law's face blanched.

Kenan approached his wife. "Catherine. Sweetheart. Sit down."

Catherine shook her head and her long red hair escaped from its loose plait and fell around her face. Kenan took her gently to the sofa and knelt before her. Rebecca reached out and grabbed at his chin then giggled as he kissed her tiny hand.

"Kenan, please, tell me what it is."

Rosie's throat tightened at the sadness in Catherine's eyes.

"Your aunt…Edie…has… She's passed on, sweetheart. The girl employed to care for your uncle William sent her brother over here to let us know. Apparently, it was quick and unexpected. It was peaceful."

"Oh…" Catherine hung her head.

Rosie bit her lip. Though she had not been well acquainted with Mrs. Montgomery herself, she knew that losing the old woman would hurt Catherine. Kenan had told Rosie that Edie Montgomery had not always been kind to her niece, but Catherine had never said a bad word about her or her uncle.

Rosie approached Catherine. "Do you want me to take her?" She gestured at the baby.

Catherine nodded and Rosie lifted the child into her arms.

"Catherine…there's one more thing."

"Yes?"

"The girl who was working for them also said that she feels unable to care for your uncle now. She said it was hard enough with Edie's help but alone, she cannot manage."

"So what shall we do?"

"I think I know someone who can help."

All heads turned to Matthew.

"What do you mean, Matthew?" Kenan got to his feet but kept his hand on his wife's shoulder.

"I know who'll be willing to take over William's care."

"Who?" Catherine stood next to her husband and took his hand.

"Huyana." The name of the young woman who had helped Catherine through her labor rolled off Matthew's tongue.

"But she has employment." Rosie rocked the little girl in her arms and leaned against Joshua as he wrapped his arms around her waist.

"Not for long," Matthew replied. "The lady she's been lodged with is leaving Virginia City to stay with an aging relative in Billings. Huyana was concerned that she'd be unable to find future employment."

"And how would you know this?" Kenan stared at his younger brother and Matthew colored.

"I've...uh...bumped into her once or twice in town."

Rosie smiled despite the tense atmosphere in the room. So Matthew had seen the pretty midwife again, had he? She suspected that it might well have been more than the once or twice he had admitted to.

"Right, well, that's settled then." Kenan nodded at Matthew. "You head into town later on to see if Huyana is interested in caring for William. Catherine, I'll get dressed then go to see to the...uh...arrangements for your aunt."

Kenan led Catherine back toward their bedroom and Rosie watched as her niece opened and closed her chubby hand at her retreating mother. At that moment, her own child moved in her womb and she placed her free hand over the swell of her belly.

Life would come and life would go. It was part of being human.

But her world was full of hope. She was married to the man she loved and expecting their child within months. Her brothers were fit and well and she had a sister-in-law and a niece she adored.

The Duggans would love whomever they would love and that was how it should be. Scars, skin tone, age, sins, past mistakes. None of them mattered in the face of true love.

About the Author

Molly Ann Wishlade has always been an avid reader and writer of stories. Her lifetime of reading has taken her from the magical worlds of The Faraway Tree and The Borrowers, to the Greek myths and legends, to Sweet Valley High and Judy Blume's Forever, to Asimov's science fiction, Jane Eyre's torment and Stephen King's masterpieces. More recently she has wandered through the vivid historicals of Philippa Gregory; the bubbly, gritty delights of Adele Parks and the fast paced thrillers of James Patterson. She loves getting lost in a novel and often regrets finishing one as the characters are usually missed like old friends. She regularly indulges her insatiable hunger for romance and passion in the delicious worlds created by romantic novelists and is working on several of her own!

What precious spare time she has is spent with her family (one gorgeous husband and two bright and beautiful children), taking long walks around the beautiful Welsh countryside (although she's still waiting for the rescue greyhound she wants to accompany her), cooking her own secret recipe curries, drinking Earl Grey (in copious amounts) and discovering delicious wines. Oh, and she also loves to ski and can't wait to go again! And buying shoes!

She wants to take readers on the rollercoaster that is life through the creation of her own characters, relationships and worlds.

She appreciates feedback, recipes and wine recommendations.

Molly loves to hear from readers. You can find her contact information, website details and author profile page at http://www.totallybound.com.

Home of Erotic Romance